PENGUIN BOOKS

WE ARE NOT ALONE HERE

O Thiam Chin is the author of three novels and six collections of short fiction including *The Dogs*, published by Penguin Random House SEA in 2020. His debut novel, *Now That It's Over*, won the inaugural Epigram Books Fiction Prize in 2015. His work has appeared in *Granta*, *The Cincinnati Review*, *Mānoa*, *The Brooklyn Rail*, *QLRS*, *World Literature Today* and elsewhere.

T0021641

We Are Not Alone Here

O Thiam Chin

PENGUIN BOOKS

An imprint of Penguin Random House

PENGUIN BOOKS

USA | Canada | UK | Ireland | Australia
New Zealand | India | South Africa | China | Southeast Asia

Penguin Books is part of the Penguin Random House group of companies
whose addresses can be found at global.penguinrandomhouse.com

Published by Penguin Random House SEA Pte Ltd
9, Changi South Street 3, Level 08-01,
Singapore 486361

Penguin
Random House
SEA

First published in Penguin Books by Penguin Random House SEA 2022

Copyright © O Thiam Chin 2022

ISBN 9789815058062

Typeset in Garamond by MAP Systems, Bangalore, India

www.penguin.sg

'... *if there was indeed a place one goes after death then it could only be a place determined by one's vision of the world; of life; of concerns. Hell is a place on earth. Heaven is a place in your head. The garden is the place I'll go if I die.*'

—David Wojnarowicz

Don't be afraid. Come closer.

Stay with me.

Don't go.

You're speaking too softly, I can't hear you. You need to speak up. It's okay, there's no one here, just you and me. You don't have to whisper. Talk to me.

What are you saying? I don't understand. What did he make you do? You had no choice in any of this? He made you do it? What exactly did he make you do? What had he said to you?

The room is dark, yes, but I can still see you, the bare outline of your body in the dim light. Your hair, so black, like spilled ink.

Come, let me see your face. Lean in a bit so I can make out your features. Yes, better, much better. Why is your face wet? No, no need to wipe it off, it's okay, I know how you feel. Are you hurt? Where are you hurting?

No, I'm fine, I don't need to move, you don't have to do that. I'm tired, that's all, very tired. Let me rest, I can just lie here. Stay with me. We can talk or sit in silence, I don't mind, either is fine. Don't worry about me. I don't need any help.

Yes, that's better, I can hear you now.

You say you have to do everything he tells you, that you always listen to him, that you only ever wanted to be his friend. Because he is—what? Why is your voice so soft again? I can't hear you. Your face has slipped into the shadows. I can't see you.

Are you scared? Why?

1

Ah, that smell in the air, so sweet and dense, so familiar. Can you smell it? Is it coming from you? I know that smell, but it hurts to breathe in too deeply, every breath is like a lump of pins down my throat.

Go ahead, you can talk to me. I'll listen. I'm a good listener. Tell me everything about him.

Did he ever tell you it would come to this one day? He did? Did he tell you everything? No? What did he tell you then?

That we are all part of it—you, me, him? Was that what he told you? Did you believe him? Every word of it? You did?

Ah, well, what can I say? We believe what we choose to believe. But I don't think I was ever a part of this, not by choice anyway. I was forced, made to choose. It didn't come easy to me, the things I had to do, the things that were put on me, alone, to bear. I had to do what I could, nothing else.

But none of it matters now, does it?

Don't make that face. I'm not dead yet. You can do that when I'm gone. It's still early, I'm still here, am I not?

Am I dying? Is this what it's like to die? Do you know what dying means?

Yes, it's rather cold, isn't it? The floor is chilly and damp beneath me. No, I don't need a blanket or anything. I'm fine. No need to fuss over me.

Can you hear that?

There, can you hear it? No?

Someone's moving around in the room. Can you see it? Is that him? Who is it? It's too dark for me to see anything.

Ah, you're keeping mum. Why do you click your tongue? Did I say something wrong?

You have to speak up. I can't hear you.

No, I didn't know this was going to happen. I didn't see it coming at all. No, I don't know anything, you have to believe me.

What? I should have known this was coming? What nonsense! As if I can see into the future. It's not like looking into a magic ball, don't be silly.

Maybe you're right. In a way, I'm not really surprised. I won't pretend any of it surprises me now. The facts are what they are, what you see and hear, I can't deny that.

So, you saw everything then? Between me and the man? No, I won't lie to you, I'm a lousy liar, I can't lie to save my life. What can I tell you? What do you need to know?

Oh, what do I remember?

I can remember the man's cold hand on mine, the sudden grip, the weight of the pressure. I remember the look on his face, the deliberate, minute adjustment of it towards something muddled, a bewildered expression, barely holding it together, his emotions roused, rising to the surface. I remember turning to look at what he had just seen behind me. You standing inside the door of our bedroom, staring in, glaring at us.

What do I not understand? What are you trying to say? Everything that had happened had something to do with me? But what exactly is my part in all this, do you know? What was it that I had done, what was wrong with any of it?

But why you? Why did I bring you into this in the first place?

Well, it's simple, really. Because of the man.

Don't be so agitated now.

Calm down, please. No need to make a scene.

Okay, better.

Now, where was I?

You're there, standing at the door, silent, watchful, like a hawk. I'd wanted to run up to you then, to snatch you away, to hide you again. How did you appear like that, so suddenly? I remember the stare you gave me, the intensity of it, the confusion and the relief and the anger in it, all mixed up. Why didn't you move or say anything? The man and I were waiting for you to do something, to give a cue or a sign, so we could, at least, make our own moves. But there you were, so still, like a block of ice, looking at me and the man, motionless.

What were you thinking then?

Ah, your laughter, so bright and robust—when was the last time I heard it? And your giggles—does anyone giggle like that anymore? What's so funny about what I have just said? Tell me. Maybe I can laugh about it, too.

Oh, the person wasn't you, the one standing there?

But if it wasn't you, then who was it? I know what I saw.

What did I really see?

I saw the man going up to you, releasing his hand from my arm, leaving a pink, ghostly imprint on my skin. I saw him rushing to you, like a man fleeing a fire, holding you in his arms, turning sharply to me, his eyes wild with incomprehension, with disbelief. *What's going on, what have you done?* You swayed your eyes from the man to me, like a pendulum. I remember feeling a fierce, irrational impulse to reach out, to touch your face, head, your arms. But you continued to give me that defiant stare, and suddenly, I wanted to slap you hard across your small, round face. To burn the mark of my palm on your smooth unsullied skin, to turn it red, to bruise it. I even imagined the sting in my palm, hot and searing, yet deeply satisfying.

What did you say? That I should have done that? Ah, but that I was too weak, that I thought too much?

Maybe I should have. But I didn't want to play your silly little game. I knew what you're doing, and I didn't want to fall for it again. You're always so wily, so cunning, like the man.

Ah, that laugh of yours, so loud, resounding off the walls, an oily slithering thing. Did I say something funny? Does all this sound like a joke to you, something ridiculous?

Me and my nonsense, you said. Am I confusing you, or just myself? You asked me what I had said to the man earlier, in the bedroom. Why did you ask? I didn't tell him anything.

No, I'm not a liar.

What do I remember from what had happened, from what the man had said to me? I can tell he was scared. His fear had a terrible stench that I could smell right off him when he came into the house. Repulsive, repugnant. He could not find the words to convey this fear. Perhaps he knew something was wrong, but what—what did he know? His voice quavered in indecision, in his inability to act or speak, like it always does when the occasion calls for it. Not a voice you want to hear when you need assurance.

Yes, maybe you're right. Like you, he's wily, tricky. He knows how to control me, to put me under his thumb. Have I always allowed it? I don't know. Things are not that simple, that clear-cut, when you've been with a person for a long time. Maybe I'm weak, as you claim I am. That I am too weak to even put up a fight. That I believe everything he tells me. That I'm too naïve, too blind.

But you're wrong.

Why are you turning your face away? You don't believe me?

Anyway, let me continue.

The man was angry and incoherent when he first arrived, barging into the house with an air of indeterminate fury, his movements livid, frantic. I had followed him from the living room to the kitchen, trying to calm him down. His eyes were wild, rabid. He was in an agitated state, tripping over his words, rushing to say everything that came to his mind. I could not pull away from him, to find the distance I needed to understand what he was saying. The man was talking too fast, flinging his words at me and making no sense.

Do I even remember a single word he said?

No, I don't.

The man had disappeared for so long before he finally decided to come around for a visit. He had charged into the house like a storm blowing in. *I need to talk to you, now.* He could not keep still, pacing the kitchen nonstop, his body charged with a coiled tension, almost irrepressible. I watched him from where I stood at the side of the marble-top island in the kitchen. I listened to the sounds coming from the other parts of the house, half anticipating to hear some noise coming from you, in the room upstairs. I had just fed you dinner, egg fried rice with char siu and anchovies, I remember. One of your favourites, right? You always kick up a fuss when you're hungry or thirsty. But you had just had your dinner, so perhaps, I thought, you would be quiet, sated.

Keeping a steady gaze on the man, I cast my mind's eye around the house, looking out for potential dangers, trying to assure myself that everything was secure, that you were safe. Sometimes you wanted to play hide-and-seek, and would expect me to go find you. It's a game you often like to play when you're bored or restless. Sometimes, you hid yourself so well that I had to call out your name, to get you to come out. You're so clever, aren't you? Sneaky little monkey.

What? I didn't try hard enough to find you when we played the game? No, I did, I searched everywhere for you. Every nook and cranny, every corner of the house. I didn't leave a single stone unturned. I was meticulous.

Ah, maybe I'd have found you if I had tried a little bit harder. Well, maybe.

But you little devil, you sure know how to deceive me.

No, perhaps I shouldn't move my head so much. Strange that it feels so heavy now, leaden, like a thing apart from my own body. So hard to even lift it off the floor. What's that at the back of my head? No, you don't have to do it, I can still move my hands. It's okay, I just need to brush the hair away from my face, it's blocking my eyes, I can't really see clearly.

No, I don't want to close my eyes. It's better like this. I can see you.

You want me to tell you everything the man told me? You want to know everything?

But I've already told you what I remember. Haven't you been listening?

I'm not the one playing the silly little game. I'm not pretending anything. Ah, not much time left, you say. But how do you know?

Do you want me to continue?

Okay.

So, the man finally vented his anger and frustration and collapsed on the floor of our bedroom, his energy spent. I knelt beside him. He was weeping openly, his head bent to my clenched fists, contrived. *I'm so sorry,* he said, repeating it like a chant. The tremors of his body entered mine, small vibrations that rattled my insides. *I love you, please don't leave me, I don't know what to do now,* he said. His words did not make any sense to me. *I won't,* I whispered, *I'm always here.*

Why did I lie to him? Did I?

Did you hear that? That sound—is it a cry or a moan? Somewhere in this room. But it's too dark to see anything. What do you see? Is it the man? Where is he now? What's going on? Can you hear him?

He's dying, isn't he?

No, I don't want him dead. Why did you say that? When have I ever wanted him dead? Stop saying that, I'm not a liar.

And stop laughing, too, will you? It's not funny at all. Stop it.

Now you're making me laugh. It hurts. My head.

Don't you remember how you used to laugh? I do. So innocent and untainted—a pure bright sound ringing in the air.

It makes one's heart swell, just to listen to it. Like an open trap, inviting, drawing in a prey. A beautiful flower, with its scent and sweet nectar, waiting to clasp its serrated jaws.

You can laugh all you want. It's true.

What else do I remember about you?

I remember you standing in the garden at the back of the house, hiding from me, but in vain. I had already seen you. You were standing absolutely still. A small black butterfly—or was it a moth?—had landed on your arm. You looked up at me in utter surprise, not moving, afraid of startling the butterfly into flight; you wanted me to look, to stay in the same spell you were in, to hold still. Can you believe this, your eyes seemed to say. It suddenly dawned on me again that you're only a child, with a child's sense of wonder and curiosity. How easy it was to forget this, your innate nature. I crouched beside you on the grass, and we were like a pair of silent, watchful beasts, waiting on something that felt like a small miracle. Time held its breath; seconds ticked away. The black butterfly stretched out its thin translucent wings, flapped, and disappeared over the high wall. You looked crestfallen, almost grief-stricken, as if your world had suddenly collapsed.

Yes, I remember that. Why did you think I would forget that?

You're always so sensitive. Too sensitive, I thought.

No, I'm not telling you what I want to remember, I'm telling you what's important, what you really need to know.

I'm not stalling for time. I have no reason to do that. I'm not going anywhere, am I?

Why is it so important for you to know what the man had said to me? What do you need to know?

But there are so many things to remember. So many memories crowding my mind, all crying to be brought to life again. My head, it feels so tight now, like it's stretched out of shape from everything I can recall. Here's what I remember: your first night in the house—how you had screamed and screamed, throwing all your strength into it, and in the end had only exhausted yourself. And the many nights that followed, sitting in the dark beside your bed, watching you sleep, the dark-blue moonlight illuminating your face, your body tucked under the Snoopy blanket. Do you remember how I'd coo to get you to sleep, *you poor thing, you poor, poor thing, I'm here, Mummy's here.*

You don't need to hear any of this? This is not important to you? Why not? Am I going round in circles?

Everything makes sense in the end.

Everything will come to an end.

But how will I get there? Where can I go?

Perhaps we can start with a place, a specific point in time, a moment. Perhaps let's start with a person. You.

Let me take a good look at you.

Your hair, a halo of frizzy ends, untameable, frames your thin, inscrutable face. You're beautiful, you know that, that doll face of yours. It's a blessing and a curse, something you can't or won't be able to shake off. I've seen the way your others, even strangers, have looked at you, patting your head, using the ends of your long, curly hair, complimenting you, your looks. Your beauty sets you apart from everyone around you, creating an impenetrable illusion of invulnerability, of aloofness, even our age, so young. Your beauty, like a hammer held against my skull, waiting for the right moment to fall.

Ah, are my thoughts going all over the place. Am I really confusing myself now?

Is that the reason I brought you here, to the house?

Do I really hate the sight of you? Why would you say that?

No, you're blameless, you did nothing wrong. You're here because I needed you here.

You don't want to hear any more of this? Why? Nothing matters?

What matters then? Does anything matter at all?

If you can only hear the voices in my head now. So many of them, all rising in pitch, wave after dark wave. It hurts to think, to move from one thought to another. And the faces snaking through the crawlspace of my mind—large, featureless, imposing. I can see them all, but I do not recognize any. Who are they?

You don't have to do that. Yes, it feels slightly better now. What you put under my head? A cushion, some rags? Good.

a moment, let me catch my breath. The pain will go away.

The faces are gone now. Except one.

boy.

it's him.

you already know him, don't you? But how?

that smile? What are you thinking? Those dimples, like ters on your lovely face, so pretty. Did you smile to him the first time?

oesn't matter? I don't need to know!

u won't tell me, but I know he's here, the boy. I can sense h can feel his presence, I can remember that smell. I haven't f ten his smell, that earthy pungent scent he gives off, as if he re pulled from somewhere deep in the ground. His smell pereates the air, like thick heavy fumes. His face is slowly forming in my head, perching at the edge of a memory, still as a butterfly. I know he is waiting for me to acknowledge him, to say his name aloud.

No, nothing's stopping me from saying his name.

But I can't, it's impossible.

Tell me. How do you know the boy?

Why are you so quiet now? You don't want to say anything? It's too late for silence. It won't get you anywhere.

The boy's face—I can still remember it very clearly. The thin arch of his feathery brows, the cherry nub of his nose, dark solemn eyes, already resigned to what life had to offer. He had demanded so little, even as a baby, hardly ever cried, you know that? It was hard to know what he wanted, if he was hungry or thirsty or needed a diaper change. When he cried, it was almost soundless, like light hiccups, but his face, no, his whole body, would turn red, a burning red, and he would break out into violent trembles, which always took a long time to subside. Holding him when he cried like that always made me very nervous, fearful, as if I were failing him in some terrible way, failing to give him what he wanted, failing to be a mother. Sometimes I got so scared that I would put him back in the cot and leave him there, alone, just for a while. Until I could get my mind back.

At other times, the boy was such a joy to behold. His smile, when he smiled, was enough to brighten up my days when the man was not around. Whenever I took the boy out, for walks or a grocery run, his eyes would never stop surveying the surroundings, turning his body this way or that, to take in everything around him. The faces of the people we passed, the buildings, the cars, the other children, flowers, cats, trees, birds. He especially liked the birds, any kind, really—sparrows, pigeons, crows, kingfishers— perhaps he liked anything that flew. He would point them out to me, his chubby finger tracing their movements, their sudden flights. I taught him the word *bird*, and in no time, he learnt how to say it, and everything was *bird, bird, bird*. Many times, he would point at me and say: *bird. Me, bird?* I would repeat, and he would scrunch up his face, a trickle of giggles escaping his mouth.

He told you about the birds as well, I see.

He had always been a quiet boy. Sometimes, I could not tell he was in the same room as me if I had left him alone for a while. He would play with his toy cars and wooden building blocks, barely making a sound. Sometimes I would even forget him when my mind drifted off elsewhere, distracted by my own thoughts. It did not happen often, but enough to make me wary of my mental wanderings. *Stay alert*, I told myself, *be here*. Stirring from these reveries, I would get up to look for the boy, wherever he was in the house. He would look at me, puzzled, perhaps even bemused, when he saw me, but never resisted when I picked him up to hug him, happy and secretly relieved that he was where he was, playing by himself. He was always an easy child to handle in this aspect, never too much of a trouble.

But I was a lousy mother, you said. Did I leave him alone because I didn't want to be bothered by him, that he demanded so much from me? What made you say that?

No, I was with him all the time. I never really let him out of my sight. I kept him with me, by my side.

Out of sight, out of mind?

No, you're wrong, it's not true. You don't understand, you won't understand. What's it like to be a mother, a new mother.

It was a tough time, having a child, taking care of one, and I was new to everything, and everything demanded all my attention, my energies. I had barely finished washing up after a meal, and a tower of filthy laundry would be waiting for me. And the boy was constantly getting himself dirty with smears of food, snot, and saliva. I had to clean up after him wherever he went, leaving behind trails of discarded toys, sweet wrappers, and half-chewed cereal. Nothing got done, all was a mess. I just couldn't keep up, no matter what I did, how hard I tried. I barely had an appetite during those days, only remembering to eat when I began to feel the sharp pangs in my stomach, an apple here, a biscuit there, nothing much of a meal, really, but it was enough to keep me going, like a machine.

That's how it felt like then—my life in automation, every cog fitting into place, turning and turning, every step, every routine carried out without fail—nothing could fail, I would not allow it. What I wanted was to keep everything together, to keep it going. I could never stop. Yet, at times, it felt like my private, inner life, the one humming quietly, desperately beneath the busy overwhelmed one, was slipping me by, ticking down to nothing. I was grinding myself down to an empty husk, ashes.

Still, the days came and went, like a stream, flowing and relentless, and I was swept up in it. All I needed to do was to keep my head up, to try to stay afloat—I simply had to stay afloat. I had to survive, for myself, for the boy's sake.

Yes, it was me who wanted the baby in the first place, I won't deny that.

Again, your silence. Are you here? Show me your face.

Why is it so hard to breathe now? Can you open the windows to let in some air?

Yes, better.

No, I don't need anything. Just stay with me. Don't go.

Did you hear that? There, there it is again. What's that over there?

Where are you going? What are you doing?

Did you move something across the floor? What were you carrying? I heard you dragging something away. What's that? And your hands, why are they so cold?

Hold mine.

Better?

Everything is so quiet now. Not a sound in the world. Why don't you say something for a change? Don't hide in the dark, your face is in shadows now, I can't make out anything. Perhaps it's me, I can't really see well, all these black spots in my vision. Let me close my eyes for a moment.

I'm still here.

Where were we? Ah, the boy.

Do you want to hear something else? I suddenly remember something. Do you want to hear it?

I remember how quiet you can be at times, how you carry the silence around, like an invisible weight. It's not a silence that is the absence of sounds, like what we have here now; no, it's something that exerts a force, like gravity, like the pull of the moon on the rise and fall of tides, very real and tangible. Your silence hums like an unseen insect buried deep in the ground. I remember the thin line of your pale lips when you choose to be silent, to stay in your own thoughts, the slight twitching along your jawline—I can see it all very clearly in my mind.

Here's another thing I remember.

The day you stepped out into the small garden at the back of the house and stood under the mango tree, your feet on the thick exposed roots. You had turned to me when I shouted at you from—where was I? Why had I left you alone? How did you manage to elude me again and again? Your face, when I came near you—again, your pursed lips, the twitching—was held in a sort of suspended animation, of disbelief. You glared at me with a look of deep suspicion, as if I were a complete stranger, before you deliberately softened your expression. Why were you alone, out there in the garden? I had always kept the glass-panelled door of the living room locked when we were alone in the house. I had warned you so many times about the things in the garden that were dangerous—I had tried to put the fear in your heart, for your own sake—that if you ventured out there alone, unsupervised, someone or something would snatch you away and eat you up. You would nod submissively every time I warned you about these dangers. *What are they?* you had asked once. *Monsters, very scary monsters*, I said, levelling my gaze at you, unflinching. Still, you never listened.

How long had you stood at the mango tree that time? It was impossible to tell. How did you find the key to unlock the living room door and walk out into the garden? How did you even know where I had kept it? Or, had I simply forgotten to lock it that morning? I shuddered to think about what you had been doing under the tree. I must have seen you. Had I fallen asleep on the sofa again? Was I in one of my spells? I can't honestly remember, but I rushed out through the tinted glass door and yelled at you. You turned slowly, as if against your will, to look at me. You were wearing the bright yellow sundress that I had recently bought for you. It stood out sharply in the shade of the tree—I had to squint to look at you—and, as I approached, I saw something falling out of your left hand. A clump of soil, which you tried to hide with your bare feet, stamping it back into the ground.

What are you doing out here? I shouted and, when you said nothing—again, that inexplicable silence—pulled at your arm and dragged you away from the mango tree, back into the house. You did not resist, though you turned back twice to look at the tree, as if you had left something behind. I made you wash your hands several times at the bathroom sink and even scrubbed out your fingernails with a brush to get rid of the soil under them. The flesh at the tip of your fingers turned red and raw, and you cried out in pain as I cleaned—I was hoping that would teach you a lesson, not to venture out into the garden without my permission. Every time you cried out and tried to pull back, I would scrub harder.

Then, to pacify you, I sat you down at the kitchen table and prepared a snack—chocolate chip ice-cream with blueberries— which you ate in tiny mouthfuls, your eyes damp and angry. Your appetite has always been good no matter your moods, and I suspect that your moods, erratic and unpredictable at times, might have led you to binge more than you wanted to—not that you seemed to be aware of it. As you ate, you stole intermittent glances out the window into the garden, at the mango tree, and I had to restrain myself not to reach out and slap you, to snap you out of it. When you were done eating, I wiped your face, took you back to your bedroom, tucked you into bed, and locked the door.

Do you remember you fell into a fever that night? Your body was burning up, forty-degree Celsius, then forty-one, and it held for a long time that night. You did not wake up when I towelled you down several times with a cold washcloth, and when you did, your eyes were dull and unfocused, too weak to even lift your head. You mumbled incoherently in your sleep, and whenever I tried to hold you, you would push me away. Whatever I fed you—a sip of water, half a Panadol—you threw up almost immediately. It seemed like everything I was doing for you did nothing to alleviate your fever. I stayed by your side through the night and only got up to rinse the washcloth or top up the glass of water. Once, in the light of the bathroom, I caught my reflection in the mirror—my bloodshot eyes, my hair in a wild mess, the lines deepening around my mouth. I could feel my eyes bobbing restlessly behind their sockets, as if they would pop out any time. I splashed handfuls of water at my tired face—I had felt terribly hot, and for a moment, I thought I, too, had caught a fever that you had somehow passed on to me.

My thoughts started to riot. I could not imagine myself falling sick, I simply couldn't. I paced the bedroom fretfully, mumbling to myself—curt and unintelligible mumbles, tripping off my tongue—part remonstration, part prayer, part gibberish, all of which barely made any sense to me. At one point, I stood at the windows and looked out into the dark garden. I could feel the strange pull of the mango tree on my attention. I stared at it; the tree was still and majestic in the inky moonlight, its leaves glistening as if radiating from within. The darkness under its canopy was full and absolute, and, for some time, I trained my eyes on a spot near the base of the tree, hoping to catch a glimpse of what was there. But there was nothing. I moved away from the window after a while, a sense of disquietude eating inside me.

Then, sometime in the middle of the night, having exhausted myself, I must have crawled into bed and fallen asleep beside you.

I can still remember the dream I had that night. It was the first time I saw the snake. It had a face that was recognizably human, though it had neither eyes nor a mouth, only a shape and a form that created such an impression. Before me, the snake slowly unfurled itself from a coil and slithered to my feet, holding its scaly head up to stare intently at me, as if giving me a thorough examination. Before I knew it, it was moving up my legs, coiling itself around my body, constricting me into a tight, though not uncomfortable, grip. It put its face right next to mine, and started to speak to me, its silky breaths landing on my skin in cool, even spurts, the forked tip of its tongue touching my lips, teasing, probing. It spoke not with words, but in an otherworldly language—something I felt rather than heard, with my skin, my instincts—that I could only understand in transitory fragments. But still, the words set off a reel of indelible images in my head—did I dream inside the dream?— which was strangely all about you.

Yes, you.

In the vision, you were always changing, your face morphing into different guises from one moment to the next, and, yet each was imprinted with your identity, your distinct features. I tried to hold on to these images but they continued to slip away from me, one swiftly replacing another, already gone.

And then suddenly I had this premonition that you'd been taken from me, that you're already dead, and the awareness of this, which echoed in a hollow shriek in the pit of my stomach, knocked the breath out of me. I started to struggle, to break the hold the snake had on me. *No, it's not possible,* I tried to scream, but nothing escaped my mouth. *I won't let it happen,* I yelled, and put all my strength into extracting myself from that death-like grip of the snake. *Please, no, not again.*

When I surfaced from the dream, from my sleep, I was in a pool of cold sweat, the sheet clasped in furious knots in my fists. I turned to you then, still sleeping next to me, lying under the blanket, your face tranquil, undisturbed, so peaceful. I put my hand to your forehead; the temperature had gone down. I dropped myself to the floor beside the bed, holding your hand, my relief breaking over me like a burst dam, and I cried for a long time.

Yes, I saw the snake. You saw it too?

I think it's a Burmese python.

I looked it up shortly after. I wanted to know what it was. I still remember the distinct patches of scales running down its back, small islands of glimmering brown.

No, I didn't have the dream again, not for some time.

It took nearly three days for you to fully recover from the fever. Even when you're well, I kept you in bed for another two days, just in case. I barely left your side, except to prepare meals for you, porridges, soups, tonics. You had wanted to get up to walk around, to play with your toys, but I strictly forbade it. I gave you books to read, but you could not keep it up for long. The meds I gave you made you drowsy and lethargic, and with nothing else to do, you took nap after nap, for hours, and sometimes, deep in sleep, you would let out a stream of dream-talk. Vague, half-formed words that added up to nothing.

Once, sitting beside you, I thought I heard you whisper the word: *snake*. Immediately I leant closer to you, unsure whether I had heard it right. Then you said it again, softer than before: *snake*. A blunt, unrestrained fear bloomed inside me, along with an irrational thought: were you having the same dream I had? Did you, too, dream about the snake, the same snake that spoke to me? Of course, the whole idea was absurd, too ridiculous. I quickly woke you up, which you did almost instantaneously, popping your eyes wide open, as if you were just pretending to be sleeping all along. I asked you about the dream, the one you just had.

What dream? you said, your voice soft, feeble. *About the snake.* You peered into my eyes and shook your head. *I don't remember*, you said. But not for a moment did I believe you then. I knew you had seen it somehow, in your dream, you must have. You're always lying, though you're not a good liar—your seams always show.

How do I know that?

From your face. I can see your lie immediately. The subtle dip of your head, your eyes dropping momentarily to the left, before raising them to check my response. Your too-bright smile.

So you had seen the snake in your dream then.

The boy showed it to you? But why?

There, that smile of yours again. So charming, so deceitful. Do you really want me to believe that? You have got to try harder.

Let's say, for a moment, I believe you. Tell me, where did the boy show you the snake?

At the mango tree? The one in the garden?

Ah, so he often appeared in your dreams, standing by the tree, with the snake? Now, now, aren't you overdoing this? Stretching the lie just a bit. How do you expect me to believe you at all?

You need to be more careful with the details when you tell a story. Especially one that you're making up on the spot. A good lie is almost always better than a half-truth, for the truth is never adequate or interesting enough to tell the whole story.

Now, let me tell you something about the mango tree.

The tree was there, right from the start. It came with the red-brick, three-storey semi-detached house we bought, along with a small Japanese-style koi pond beside it. The previous owners, a Chinese couple in their early sixties, had planned to migrate to Hong Kong to live with their only daughter who had just had her first child, their first grandson, and they were in a hurry to sell the place. The house had only been put on the market for a week, and already there were several parties interested in it, according to the realtor who showed us around the place. It was generally well-kept—the wife was a full-time homemaker—though it exhibited clear signs of wear and tear: the yellowing wallpaper in the master bedroom, curling at the corners; the brown water stains on the bathroom ceiling; the crack-lines trailing across the kitchen walls. Still the price was within our budget, and the location was a catch, situated in the eastern edge of a new housing estate, on a quiet street lined with tall Angsana trees.

We had recently come into some money, after the man was headhunted and hired by a blue-chip advertising agency as their creative director, a role that came with a better-than-expected pay raise and a sign-on bonus. I had been staying in a one-room flat, owned by my late mother, for as long as I could remember, and the man had wanted me to move into a bigger, better place, one with a quiet environ and maybe a small garden. After viewing the house, we were more or less in agreement that it was very close to what we wanted, and so he made the down payment and bought the house for me. *Now you can start a new life*, he said, *and it's a new start for us, too.*

I still remember the mango tree at our first viewing—we had two viewings, the latter a more thorough one, to more or less confirm our decision—looking down at it from the balcony of the master bedroom on the second floor. In the late afternoon sun, the tree was huge and imposing, its dark-green canopy extending over the koi pond, its fleshy gnarled roots breaking up the surface of the earth. It took up nearly a third of the garden, and from time to time a bird would dart out of the tight cluster of leaves and branches, in nervous flight, as if released from its clutch. I was drawn to it instantly, and when I had the chance—the man was talking to the realtor about some defects in the kitchen—I unlocked the glass-panelled door at the back of the living room, slipped off my ballet flats, and walked to the tree, my bare feet cooled by the patch of trimmed grass. The shade under the tree was unexpectedly chilly, as if the thick canopy had cut off the heat of the sunlight entirely, the sensation not unlike entering the embrace of a cocoon of cool air. I looked up and was surprised to see the green nubs of mango dangling off the branches. Was it mango season? A surge of pleasure welled up inside me; to own such a tree, a fruit-bearing one no less, was nothing less than a thing of pride, a gift of unsought serendipity. I'd gladly eat every single fruit that comes from it, I thought. I closed my eyes and dug my toes into the dirt, relishing the idea of a future happiness, a deep indulgence.

It was only when I heard voices coming from the house that I finally opened my eyes. The man was calling out for me, but somehow I didn't move or respond to him. I was still suspended in a spell under the tree, and I didn't want to break out of it. His voice grew louder, more impatient. From where I stood, I could see the shadows moving behind the tinted windows, unable to differentiate between the man's and the realtor's. I watched as the shadows moved from one part of the living room to the next. When the realtor threw open the doors that led to the garden, she let out an audible gasp, her hands rising to her chest, as if my appearance under the mango tree had caught her by surprise.

There she is, the realtor said, composing herself, and turning to address the man behind her, *still enjoying the view*. The man emerged and stood at the edge of the worn parquet floor of the living room, his face bearing traces of irritation.

What are you doing there under the tree? he yelled across the short distance.

Enjoying the view, I said, remembering to tag a smile at the end of my words, and started walking back to the house, to join the man.

I slipped on the flats, the grits of sand rubbing not uncomfortably against the soles of my feet. I didn't tell him anything about the mangoes on the tree or the calm I felt standing there, alone and solitary, in its inviting shade.

Three months later we moved in. I had taken a long break from my work as a freelance copywriter, turning down new assignments, to oversee the whole renovation of the house. It was during this period that the mangoes came into maturation, turning from green to a warm shade of canary-yellow, weighing down the branches. The tree was near to bursting with mangoes, and had shaken off the early fruits to the ground with a prolific, uninhibited indifference. Thus abandoned, they were swiftly attacked by rivalling hordes of black ants and flies, reducing them in no time to greying lumps of pulpy flesh and mangy loose skin. Once, armed with a pair of metal tongs, I spent a whole morning picking up the loose-skinned carcasses—some livid with maggots, resembling wriggling bits of rice—that often came apart at the slightest of touch. The air was scented with a putrid, stale-saccharine stench of cloying rot that never seemed to dissipate, even after I had removed all the decomposing mangoes.

Once I cleared the mess, I took the wooden step-ladder, garden shears and a large woven basket—items the previous owners had left behind in a storeroom for such a purpose—and climbed up the tree and began harvesting the mangoes.

Each mango I picked was at least half a size bigger than my palm, and I had to make a few trips up and down the ladder to empty the contents of the basket onto the grass patch, which gradually grew into a sizeable pile. The ladder, even when fully extended, did not allow me to reach the highest branches of the tree, where clusters of mangoes beckoned with full, succulent ripeness. I had contemplated scaling the branches to get to these far-flung fruits, but gave up the idea shortly after, not trusting my climbing skills or the dexterity required to manage the shears and basket all at once. I'd have to leave them to fall from the tree naturally if the birds did not get to them first.

Later, when I took my first bite of a peeled mango, plunging my fingers into the firm, juicy flesh and peeling off a sliver of it, the taste was like an explosion of sweetness in my mouth—dense and overwhelming, irresistible. I ate and ate until I couldn't eat it any more that first time, my whole body sated by the overindulgence.

Oh, you hated the mangoes, didn't you? But they're not as disgusting as you made them out to be. You're just too spoilt. You won't know a good thing even if it was right in front of you the whole time.

What's out there? What are you looking at? Is there someone there? Tell me what you see.

Nothing? Can't be nothing.

Who is out there?

Ah, the boy told you he likes mangoes? That he found them sweet? Yes, of course, I remember that. I know he likes to eat them. I would often add mango to his favourite foods, cereal, yoghurt, ice-cream, oatmeal. Like me, he can eat mangoes all day long.

He's not a fussy eater like you. He would eat anything I gave him.

Tastes don't change. You don't know him like I do.

Why that snicker on your face? You don't believe me?

There's that buzz in my head again, the voices, the noises. Did I tell you they rarely go away? They silence all the other sounds in my head. I hear them all the time, one or another, sometimes in a loud muddle.

Just give me a moment. They'll go away.

You would be surprised to know, but I can still feel the presence of the boy around me, even now—perhaps I mean to say that I can still sense him somehow. The kind of thing you can sense when you step into an exact spot that someone has just vacated, the particular smell of that person that still lingers in the air, an aura that has yet to be displaced. Have you ever experienced that before? I would step into a place—the boy's bedroom, the bathroom—and immediately I could feel his presence, deeply familiar, unmistakable, as if he were there just moments ago. The feeling was uncanny at first, though it never bothered me. I would then proceed to search the room carefully, for something he might have left behind, anything that would tell me he was there, briefly. A strand of hair, a stain on the wall, finger marks—anything would have sufficed, I thought. But there was nothing.

Still, I hope, for I know what I believe is true—that he's never gone. Some part of him is still alive, still making his presence felt, in the house, around me.

I'm not mad, I know that, I'm not dreaming this up. A mother has a sense of these things; it comes naturally, a native instinct.

Once, while packing up some old clothes in the boy's bedroom, I felt the indelible sensation of someone standing behind me, at the door, watching. I turned my head just in time to see a tail-flicker of shadow disappearing across the surface of the door. I got up and ran out of the room, racing down the corridor, peeking into all the rooms. I paused at the top of the stairs, a volley of thoughts wheeling in my head. The air around me was stagnant, heavy with a sweet, milky smell that I knew must have come from the boy. *You're here, you're here,* I had said, as if by uttering these words aloud I was bringing him back, making him real again. I stood there, taking breath after breath, long and deep, trying to breathe everything in. The stairs in front of me started to spin—a sudden scene zipped across my mind: the tilt and the tumble, the fall, endless, unstoppable—and I immediately shut my eyes, trying to block out what my mind was racking up, an old reel of scenes. But there was no stopping it.

For a while after that incident, I was alert to whatever was going on in the house, every sound, every movement, every shadow. I did not go out—I could not bear to be out there, in the company of other people, the bright, abrasive chatter, the heat and messy din of human contact—and kept myself within the confines of the house. The house was my sanctum, a barricade against whatever was out there, trying to sneak in, to infiltrate my thoughts. Sitting at the dining table or lying on the sofa or bed, keeping myself as still and quiet as possible, I could hear all the noises the house was making, the ticks and knocks and light hums, as if there were a creature hidden and living within the walls, making its presence felt. I'd stay absolutely silent, listening, trying to decipher these sounds, to tell them apart. Sometimes I'd rise and trace the source of an unknown sound, from wall to wall, moving from room to room, hopeful it would lead me somewhere, perhaps to the very thing I was searching for.

What was I looking for? What do you think? Surely you must know already.

For any sign that would let me know the boy is alive, present, here in the house. I know he's still around. That he's not gone.

Yes, like you say, he's always here.

But I can't see him.

You see him all the time? How, where?

But you don't know him, you've never seen him before. How would you know what he looks like?

Yes, I'll calm down, I won't get too excited. You don't have to do that, to wipe the spit off my chin. It doesn't matter. You don't have to tell me to breathe. I'm not an idiot.

Okay, I feel much better now.

What do you mean he wanted to play with you? Wanted to be friends with you so you can play together? Did he really say that? That he would tell you everything if you're friends?

Don't make me laugh. You think I'd believe this? Good try, though.

Okay, where was I?

Let me continue.

After a period of bed rest after your fever, you were back to your usual self, cheerful and effervescent, playing with your dolls, setting up imaginary parties for them. You would chase me away with a *this is not for grown-ups!* if I ever wanted to join in or watch you enact these childish games. I'd leave you alone, but from behind the ajar bedroom door, I would hear you issue invitations to the dolls and boss them around, in a mock adult voice, telling them where to sit and when to drink their juices or milkshakes, warning them not to spill a drop. Often you would take on different voices for the dolls, varying and exaggerating them in pitch and tenor, and conduct long, meandering conversations among these dolls. Sometimes you would even break into a laughter when you pretended that one of the dolls said something funny or did something naughty. Once or twice, I overheard you reprimanding the dolls for spilling their juices and making a huge mess in a loud and threatening voice, which, after I thought about it, cleverly mimicked mine. What a clever girl. You never got tired of imagining all sorts of scenarios for your parties. Where you got your ideas, I have no clue.

And then one morning, I was walking past your room, putting away the laundry, and I heard you talking in a voice that wasn't like the one you usually employed while playing with your dolls. Gentle and polite, as if you were actually talking with someone, having some sort of an intimate conversation. I peeped in, and there you were, seated at one of the chairs around the small round table, your body turned to the side, your right hand in the air, caught in mid-motion. You looked at me in pure alarm and quickly brandished a nervous smile, then lowered your head.

Hello.

What are you doing?

Playing.

I looked around the table, at the blank-eyed dolls sitting on their tiny chairs, rigid and silent. There was a spread of colourful miniature cups and plates and cutlery, neatly arranged in front of each doll. You were dressed in a new Hello Kitty t-shirt I had bought for you, the front of it stained with dry spots of orange juice. You sneaked a glance to your side—an empty chair, the ragged teddy bear had toppled to the floor, face down—and gave a small nod. I pretended not to notice this. Instead I picked up the bear and set it upright on the chair.

Do you need anything, dear?

Nope, thanks.

You began moving the cups around, pouring another round of imaginary drink from a white plastic flask, performing the task delicately, showily. You were impatient to get back to your game, and seemed puzzled—annoyed?—at my lingering presence in the room. You cricked your head up, your mouth pulled into a pucker. I squatted down and stroked your hair, cupping a side of your face with my palm. It felt warm—was it the beginning of another fever? I touched your neck and arms to make sure, but you pulled sharply away from me.

What are you doing?

Just checking. Are you feeling okay?

I'm okay.

Still I could not bring myself to leave the room just yet. I got up and, in the bid to buy myself more time, began folding the blanket on your bed and picking up the scattered toys and books on the floor, putting them back onto the shelves and into crates. Your gaze stayed on me the whole time as I moved around the bedroom, and twice I caught you cocking your eyebrow at the teddy bear next to you, as if both of you were sharing a complicit secret.

Five more minutes and I want you to put all this away, you hear?

Okay.

I stepped out of the room eventually, and from behind the half-closed door I heard you letting out a shot of suppressed giggles before quickly hushing up.

Oh, you could sense that I was still behind the door? Smart girl.

Who was there with you?

I should know by now? No, I'm not playing dumb. I need to hear it from you.

It's not possible.

Anyway, right after that, I kept my eyes on you all the time. Tried to keep you within my sight, but it seemed you were always finding new ways to get away from me, to do your own thing. You'd play in the living room when I gave you permission, and barely had I turned away and you'd be gone, disappeared. Maybe that's how the hide-and-seek game came about, me going in search for you and you hiding from me. The house was big and spacious, three-storey high, and while I knew every nook and corner, there were still spots that allowed for a child to hide herself well, if she knew how to.

I would patiently search for you, going from floor to floor, room to room, while keeping in the spirit of fun and indulging a child's foolish game. At first, it was easy to find you, hiding under a rack in a storeroom or inside an old disused cupboard. You always appeared visibly distraught whenever you were found, your face darkly cast with undisguised anguish and frustration. Later, the game became altogether different, tougher, and it seemed you were trying a lot harder to hide yourself, to find spots in the house that could accommodate your small frame and size, tight narrow spaces you could squeeze into. You had also taken the opportunity to move around when I was searching for you, going from one hiding spot to another, to escape from me. From the corner of my eye, I would catch a fleeting shadow, flitting down a corridor or slipping into a room, and go in pursuit, only for the lead to suddenly go cold. Occasionally, I would hear a noise or a sigh of laboured breath—as if you had been running and were catching your breath—in one of the rooms, but upon checking every possible hiding spot in it I'd turn up nothing. Had I imagined these noises then?

The searches took longer and longer, and I soon lost the patience for it. To cut the game short, I would call out to you and ask you to come out, saying that I had given up. I would keep my voice level, unruffled, as if this sort of thing was of no consequence. I kept it up for as long as it took, for I knew sooner or later you would get bored or distracted, and come out from wherever you were hiding. True to form, you would usually emerge, after a time, wearing a sheepish grin on your flushed face, raring for another round. When I reached out to touch you—more to assure myself than you—I could feel the heat rising from your body—always, the threat of a new fever—and start to fuss over you, wiping your face down with my sleeves or a cold towel, or sitting you down at the kitchen table with a cup of Milo or a Marie biscuit. After all, you needed your rewards, for your victories, for your ability to deceive me, and it was easy to fuel your fantasy, your self-deception.

Once, you had refused to step out from your hiding place after I sounded out my surrender and, later, a stern warning. I went into every room—my patience sapped dry and my panic rising—and yelled for you to come out. But you weren't in any of the rooms or the usual spots I would normally find you. I was at the edge of my anger when I heard your voice coming from the bottom of the stairs, soft and rattled. I ran down the staircase, seized you by the shoulders and shook you hard, shrieking into your face: *Stop it, stop playing when I tell you to. Don't make me…*

But you looked at me with a strange baffled expression on your face, your features darkening.

But I heard you. I came out when you told me to. I've been calling out to you.

No, you didn't. I'd have heard you.

You tilted your head then, and were about to mouth something before you held back. Your large eyes brimmed with tiny beads of tears. You glanced at something behind me for a second, momentarily distracted, and your body suddenly froze. I turned back and looked: the empty kitchen. You swiftly asked to be excused, and, because there was no way I would have managed the situation without rousing myself into a greater state of agitation I let you go. You ran up the stairs, escaped into your bedroom and closed the door. In the renewed silence of the house, I heard a rustle of sounds coming from your room—voices? cries?

What were you doing in the room?

He told you to ignore me, is it? That that's how I am when I'm in one of my strange moods? How could he possibly know? He's only a kid.

Quit your smile, will you?

You don't see or know him like I do, you hear me?

No, I didn't make him up in my head, I didn't have to. He's always here, as real as you and me. You would never understand what this means to me, his constant presence in the house.

No, you're the one who created him out of nothing. You made him up to get to me.

You and your make-believe games.

You can't fool me.

I knew the boy even before he was born. From before he came into being, inside me. Even before the doctor told me the sex of the baby I knew it would be a boy. I had had long vivid dreams before that, in the early months of my pregnancy—before I finally told the man the news—of a boy rising from the bloody cut-up slit of my huge stomach, howling, his face red, his tiny fists raised, as if in heated, helpless protest. I could remember his howls—how piercing they sounded, how unearthly, as if they were issued by a frightened beast that had been ripped out of a dark airless place. How terrible they had seemed, resounding in my ears. Yet through these dreams, I soon grew accustomed to these howls, which I took to be a clear, unambiguous sign that the boy would grow up to be someone special. The boy would grow inside me and then come into the world. And he would be my son.

Like a dream fulfilled, the boy slipped into the world, my world, a small bloody bundle of pink wrinkled flesh, after nearly sixteen hours of labour, though unlike in my dreams, he hardly made a sound, emitting only a series of soft hiccups. He had a full head of hair, his eyes and mouth mere cuts on a smooth, placid face. His eyes, when he finally opened them, shone with a secret, uncomplicated knowledge. He stared at me long and hard, in full assessment, and, in return, I assured him with a tight hug a safe and constant place in my heart, one that's always filled with love, with undiminished light. I kissed his soft cheeks and inhaled every scent wafting from his tiny, fragile body.

I can still remember the sweet, milky smell of his body. He never really lost this particular smell of his, even as a young boy growing up. How I loved to lean in and bend my head to his body, to his neck, and take in long, unbroken breaths of his particular scent. How it never failed to rouse up certain strong feelings in me, feelings of warmth and security and completeness. The whiff of innocence, of unsullied goodness. The smell never went away, and standing in his bedroom, I could sometimes imagine him present, just beside me, still the seven-year-old boy I had held in my arms.

He's not the same boy anymore? How do you know?

To me, he'll always be that boy. He would never change.

What do you want to know?

What really happened that day? But which day?

Why do you want to know?

Of course, I remember everything.

This is what happened.

The front door of the house was unlocked that day. I must have forgotten to lock it, coming back from a grocery run with the boy. He had run into the house ahead of me, hot and sweaty, discarding his sandals as he went, clamouring for a cold drink. I told him to wash his hands at the kitchen sink while I started clearing away the bags of food into the fridge and pantry. I offered the boy a packet of Ribena and steered him into the living room. It was late afternoon, and I was feeling tired from the short trip to the supermarket in our neighbourhood. The boy dragged out a crate of toys—Matchbox cars and trucks, broken fighter planes, disjointed fragments of a train set—from his bedroom into the living room and was attempting to assemble the railway tracks, while I watched a cooking show on TV, keeping the volume at mute.

I don't know how long it took before I fell asleep, slipping into a nap on the sofa. But when I woke up later, the cooking programme was over—it was showing some Mandarin-dubbed Taiwanese drama serial and the boy was no longer playing near the console table, though the train set was fully assembled with tracks that ran around in loops. At first I called out to the boy, thinking he might be in his room, but there was no response. I went to check his room, and when I could not find him there, I searched the other rooms, my thoughts already starting to go awry. I shouted out his name over and over again, throughout the house, but did not get a reply. When I finally saw the unlocked front door, I knew instantly what the boy had done. I ran out of the house, noting the boy's missing sandals, and found the metal gates unlatched, the bolt pulled back.

My panic rose like churning waves, slamming against my constricted chest—where could the boy go? The one-way street was empty, not a single soul in sight. Maybe he had gone to the neighbourhood park; in the car, on our way back from the supermarket, he had pointed out the swings there and said he wanted to play on it. I fled in the direction of the park, my slippers slapping loudly in the quiet air, my skin breaking into a suit of cold sweat. There was a boy on the swing, but it wasn't him—the Filipino maid who was with the child had leapt up from a nearby bench in alarm when she saw me approaching the boy, and put her hands protectively around him, throwing me a long, suspicious glare.

I left the park in haste and backtracked to the house, my mind paralysed with fear. I checked my watch—the boy could not have gone far. Maybe he had got tired and gone back home. But his sandals were still missing when I looked in. I ran down the road, in the opposite direction, calling out his name. An elderly woman peeked out of one of the houses, a watering can in her hand, and, when I stopped to ask whether she had seen the boy, had pointed towards the end of the road, issuing a string of rapid-fire Cantonese. Picking up my pace—small welts were forming where the straps had rubbed against my skin—I allowed myself the smallest glimmer of hope that the boy had just wandered off, that he was safe. I did not dare to go any further—to push my luck—till I found him.

At the end of the road was a man-made canal, two-metre or so deep. The gushing water was muddy-brown from the sudden downpour that morning, and from the construction of a new condominium taking place nearby. I clutched the rust-pockmarked railing and swept my gaze along the length of the canal in both directions. Except for a trio of sparrows perched on the opposite railing, there was no other sign of life. Seized with panic, I began scanning the water for the boy—perhaps he had fallen in?

Something a stone's throw away caught my eyes—a knot of hair?—and I ran towards it to check—a tangled mass of dead weeds caught between fallen branches.

After that, in my fired-up imagination, every object that floated on the surface of the water began to resemble parts of a body—a hand in a half-clutch, the sloping hunch of a shoulder, a pair of feet pointing skyward—and it became harder to differentiate one thing from another. I held my breath and dared myself each time to take a closer look as I walked down a stretch of the canal, and was fleetingly rewarded with a sharp stab of relief when I was mistaken. I called out the boy's name again and again, my voice turning hoarse, but still nothing.

I walked farther down the canal, all the time keeping my eyes peeled on the swift-moving currents. Then I saw it: floating at the side of the canal, near a tunnel hole, an arm arched awkwardly out of the water, motionless. It was him, the boy, I knew, a sharp instinct hitting me right in the gut. I stumbled towards it, even while something was telling me to run in the other direction, to deny what I had seen. Yet, the need to know was too overwhelming, and as I drew nearer and looked down, I saw that it was indeed the boy, his head face-down, submerged in the water, his arm crooked to his side.

I leapt off the concrete parapet of the canal, the currents hitting me hard in the face as I landed. The water was fearfully frigid, and I struggled for a while to find a proper footing. My mind was barren, barring any thought. Then, making my way forward, dragging my feet through the currents with slow leaden steps, I reached out and touched the boy's shoulder, his arm. His body was cold and stiff, unyielding.

Was he already dead when I found him?

Yes.

I disentangled the boy's arm from the sodden clump of flotsam, and raised his body out of the water into my arms. He was so heavy, so unwieldy, as if he had been weighed down by something other than water. His eyes were half-shut, his lips a dark shade of purple-blue. Trickles of silty water leaked out of his mouth as I heaved his head onto my shoulder, pushing my way to the flight of steps. His body clung to mine, solid and hefty like a wet sandbag. I did not believe for an instance that he was gone, my mind refusing to give in to the fear, to this knowledge.

Against the ferocious pull of the water, I clamoured up the steps till I reached the top and collapsed onto the grass patch, cold and breathless, lapping up gulps of air. Immediately, I attempted to resuscitate the boy, pumping his chest repeatedly, trying to get my breaths into him. I extracted the mud clogging his nostrils and slapped his face a few times, but he did not respond. I gathered him up again, wrapping my body around him, keeping his face to my chest, and slowly hobbled my way home. With every painful step I took, I kept only one thought—my only thought—alive in my head: *He's with me now, he's safe, I'll keep him safe.* It's the only thought that kept me going.

Back at the house, in the boy's room, I laid him on the bed and performed another round of CPR on him, forcing his mouth wide apart, breathing deeply into him. No response, nothing. I stripped him bare of his wet clothes and wiped him down with a bath towel, trying to rub some heat into his cold skin. The towel turned yellow in no time; grits of sand and mud had entered every part of the boy's body—nose, ears, mouth, armpits, between his legs—and it seemed the boy, fashioned entirely out of these elements, was slowly coming apart in my hands.

Yet, I did not stop—I could not; for I knew that if I ever stopped, the boy would slip away from me, and I would lose him forever. I got a new towel and kneaded his body even harder, putting all my strength into every rub. His head remained slumped on his shoulder, limp, lifeless. I cleaned around his eyes, cleared out the grains of sand from his nose, dug out the mud from under his fingernails; I wrapped his body in a thick blanket, leaving only his face exposed, like how I did when he was just a baby, to keep his body in a tight cocoon, to keep him warm. I kept uttering these words in my head: *wake up, wake up, wake up.*

Why didn't I call the ambulance then? Why didn't I think to call for help?

It didn't occur to me at all. I thought I could do everything to bring him back. He was only in the water for a short while, maybe he was still in shock, maybe he had fallen asleep and would wake up sooner or later. Maybe he was pretending to be angry with me, for not coming to him earlier, to save him, maybe he was just playing his pretend-games.

Yes, he also had his pretend-games.

When the boy did not want to go to school, he would lie in bed and pretend to be sick or deep in sleep. And I'd play along, feigning to be surprised and later flustered that I could not get him to wake up, no matter how hard I tried. *Wake up, wake up, my little prince*, I'd cry out, running my fingers down his face, along his waist. He would hold himself resolutely still—though you could feel the rising tension in his body, almost ready to burst—while I engaged in an elaborate song-and-dance about how my little boy was lost to the world, cast in an unbreakable spell by a horrible, wicked witch, and would anyone please help me wake him up.

Then, to end his ruse, I would plunge my face into his stomach—the babyish smell of his body, deepened by sleep and sweat, never failed to pierce me with such longing—and blow a raspberry, causing him to erupt into roaring laughter. Ah, the sound of his laugh—it's the most beautiful thing I've ever heard, the truest and purest sound in the whole world.

Did I think he was pretending then?

Yes.

I sat beside the bed and looked at the boy's face, his eyelids half-closed. Any time now, his eyes would pop open, I thought, and he would tell me he was hungry or thirsty, and I would bring him anything he wanted. I stayed by his side the entire time, afraid of leaving him even for a moment. I put my head on his chest and stomach, blowing raspberries, and waited for him to break into a laugh, to end the silly game.

Still, he did nothing. I studied his silent, impassive face. There were webs of cuts and scratches on his cheeks, and some wounds were weeping a blood-milky pus, which I wiped away with a clean towel. A long deep cut ran across his forehead, a clean split that opened into two flaps, revealing the dark-red flesh within. I went to get the first-aid kit and applied an antibacterial cream on the open wound, covering it with a strip of gauze. The blood rose up and stained it almost immediately. I watched it seep across the white gauze, darkening and spreading; I ripped it off and applied a new strip. The blood would stop flowing, eventually, I told myself. The wound would close up and it would heal. The body always knows how to heal itself.

What? What are you saying? That I'm crazy? That I was out of my mind?

Sorry, I didn't mean to laugh.

No, I didn't.

I don't understand what I had done, is that it? That I couldn't see a single thing?

But I saw the boy, he was right there, on the bed, right in my sight. I didn't leave him alone. I was with him all along.

No, it's the truth, what I'm telling you. Why would I make all this up? What would I get from telling you lies?

Stop interrupting me.

Shut up.

Just listen.

I cleaned the other cuts on his face, worried that they too would be infected, if left unattended. I cleared out the tiny grits of sand from them and applied the antibacterial cream, and all the while, watching his eyes, waiting for something to happen, for him to register the slightest of gestures. Even as I was treating the cuts, I could sense, in a deeper part of me, an unexpected bud of rage slowly growing, throwing out tender roots, swelling. And before I could get a hold of it, I gripped the boy's shoulders and started lashing out at him: *Stop playing! You stupid boy! Stop this game now, you hear me! If not, you'll get it from me later! Stop this nonsense.*

I raised my hand and slapped the boy across his right cheek. His whole head swerved to the side with the impact of the slap, his mouth falling open. A trail of muddy saliva dripped from a corner of it.

Stop it now.

My whole body trembled from what I had done, and it was only seconds later that I finally registered everything, the extent of my actions and what had truly happened.

Why was I so angry?

Because I thought the boy was still playing, still pretending, after all that I had done for him. That he was being very disobedient, and testing my patience.

That wasn't the real reason? How would you know?

No, I was angry and tired of his pretend-games. Sick with all the worrying.

Ah, your face, why the frown again? You're too young to be frowning all the time. What do you not understand about any of this?

Come closer, let me take a good look at you.

Did I ever tell you that your eyes are your best features? They reveal all your moods, your feelings. I don't think you can ever hide anything from anyone.

Why am I always so angry?

I don't know how to answer that.

Anyway, let me continue, please.

So I turned away from the boy for a moment, to collect my senses, my thoughts. I walked to the bedroom window. The sky was already dark by then, a smooth velvety blue, fading at the far horizon. I glanced down at the mango tree in the garden, its outline etched against the background of the falling dusk, stark and black and immense. I thought about the mangoes hanging from the branches—they're already in season, ripe and heavy— and remembered the tart sweetness of the flesh.

Then my stomach turned at the recollection, as if suddenly repulsed by the taste. Bile churned inside me, turning thick and sour. I wanted there and then to pluck every fruit off the tree and smash them on the ground, grinding the flesh to a dirty pulp with my feet. I had never hated anything so much, and it made me sick even to think about it. I closed my eyes, suppressing my nausea, my breaths rough and ragged, and pushed aside the thought. Then, after a few minutes, suitably calmed, I turned back to the boy and adjusted his head on the pillow, straightening out the curls on his forehead to cover the now disinfected wound. The gauze was tainted pink, the blood seeping through. I laid my palm on his cheek and continued my watch over him for the night.

Why? Why did you say that?

Am I remembering things wrongly? Making things up as I go along?

How would you know this was not exactly what had happened? You weren't there, you know nothing, so don't pretend you know otherwise.

Am I very confused now?

Am I confusing you?

I'm trying to piece everything together the best I can, to let you know the whole story. Isn't that what you want?

It's really that simple.

I'm not being frank or truthful? What would you know about truth?

I know myself well enough, and one thing I know for sure is that you're not real. The boy should be the one here, not you. You don't belong here, I brought you here, I fed you, I kept you alive.

No, I don't need you to keep me alive.

I don't care.

My head is killing me. Just go away and leave me alone, for a moment, please.

I don't care what will happen if you leave. You're not here because of me.

Go, just go.

You intend to stay till the end?

But what will happen in the end?

I have to tell the full story?

But the only story I have is the one in my head. And you don't believe a single word of it.

Stop, please.

I know you're still here, still listening.

What am I waiting for?

At some point in the night, I fell asleep, seated there beside the bed, despite my best effort to stay awake. I had felt something touch my ear—a feather-light pressure—and woken with a start. My first thought was that the boy had come to, and that he was trying to get my attention. The bedroom was in semi-darkness, pale moonlight streaming in, and I quickly turned to switch on the tableside lamp. The boy was still calmly in repose, not a strand of hair out of place. I held the back of my hand against his cheek; it was cold. I rubbed it for a moment, and stopped.

The thought finally became clear to me, like scales falling off my eyes. Perhaps that was the first time I knew that it was all over—the boy was truly gone—and realized what I was up against, the full unvarnished knowledge of the loss. The thought itself was unbearable, a terrible thing of slick and ungraspable proportions, and, yet somehow, it had slipped inside me, carved out a niche and then nestled itself snugly inside me. How is it that we can take and take and take, and still carry on with our lives? No matter what happens to us, we simply endure these losses, these absolute, senseless things. The thought stayed lodged and remained so for some time as I looked at the body, which was no longer a thing I associated with anything living or belonging to the boy, but as a lifeless object cast off, unwanted. I sat on the edge of the bed and did not look at the boy anymore.

Time passed, and the light outside turned bleak, darker. I finally forced myself to leave the bedroom and head down to the living room. The whole house was hollow and silent in the middle of the night, and I wanted to stay in the silence forever. I looked out the full-length glass windows into the garden, and again the sight of the mango tree came into view. I stared past it to look into the night sky.

Standing motionless in the living room, it was easy to feel that I was part of everything around me, that all that was required of me was to be very still and not think, to erase every thought from my head. I was the Edward Hopper's Nighthawks poster on the wall, the beige sectional sofa in front of the Samsung TV, the Brio train set still intact on the floor, the terracotta jar filled with green stoebe in the corner of the room: an object and its shadow, fixed and motionless. I held myself upright, straightened my back, and kept my arms beside me. I was a statue, stony and hard, unyielding, bloodless.

The moment finally, eventually, lapsed, and I knew I had to do something. I took a bunch of keys from the top drawer of the kitchen cabinet, went up to the boy's bedroom and locked it without taking another look. Then, as if a crack of light had opened up a new perspective in my vision, one that ushered in a greater self-awareness, it dawned on me that I was still wearing the same set of clothes from the day before, streaked with dirt and blood and countless stains. I darted into the bathroom in my bedroom, peeling off every shred of clothing and running scalding hot water over my body. After a long, thorough shower, I gathered all the dirty clothes in a grocery bag and threw them into the blue trash bin outside the house. Then I started clearing the train set from the floor, gathering all the parts into the toy crate and putting them in the storeroom beside the kitchen. Whoever I was, barely an hour ago, was a complete stranger to me, someone who no longer existed.

So where was the man, you said? Where was he in all this? Did I tell him anything?

Why didn't I call him?

Why should I call him?

Well, he did not come home that night. He had left a few messages on my phone, which I finally decided to check. Something about a product campaign for a big client he needed to finish up, that he was spending the night at the office. I deleted the messages after reading them. It was something I was used to, or had made myself get used to—him being not around all the time. It was better not to ask further or to know more.

Why? I don't want to get into this.

Stop asking why.

Not now, please.

When did he know?

The man came home late the following night, around eleven, and I was there at the door to greet him. I had the dinner ready—fried rice with a slab of pork chop, an egg sunny-side-up, a simple enough fare that the man liked; he enjoyed all kinds of grilled and deep-fried food and was never one to control his appetite. *All diets are bullshit*, he once told me, taking me to a steakhouse restaurant during one of our earlier dates. He sat down at the dining table and I began to serve him the food, reheated in the microwave as it had already gone cold for several hours. The man ate heartily, tearing the pork chop apart with his greasy fingers and taking huge bites, chewing in an ugly, exaggerated manner. I sat in the chair next to him, sipping a glass of chilled Moscato.

You want some, I asked him, tilting the glass at him.

Nah, too sweet for my liking, he said.

When he was done eating, he pushed away the plate, belched, and asked: *How's the boy today?*

I looked at him, smiled, and said: *Quiet, as usual.*

Why are you laughing? What's so funny now?

Stop it, or I won't continue.

So, finishing up my wine, I cleared the dirty dishes from the table and brought the man a can of Carlsberg. He drank it all up in a few lusty gulps. Once he was satiated, he began to loosen up, to talk more freely. When he wanted to, the man could be voluble and indulgent, gregarious even, generous with his teasing and flattery. We talked about the advertising campaign he was busy with—the one that had kept him away from home the previous night—and the people involved in it, the project team, names that I was familiar with, either from hearing him talk about them all the time, or from photographs he had shown me on his mobile, taken at office functions and events.

He talked mostly while I listened. I brought him another can of Carlsberg, which he emptied in no time. I could tell he was still feeling the buzz of being on his feet the whole day, his body pumped with the excitement of ideas and executions and sign-offs, though his eyes were red-rimmed and his eye-bags darker, more pronounced. I watched him closely and smiled from time to time, at appropriate moments.

No, I didn't tell him anything then. The timing wasn't right.

What's a right time?

I don't know. But it's not that moment.

The man got so drunk that night that he did not check in on the boy, which was something he usually did no matter how late he came home. I helped him to our bedroom, his body leaning sluggishly against mine, and he fell into bed and was asleep

instantly. I stroked his face, rough with new stubble, and the face
of the boy came to mind, involuntarily, uninvited. The boy's nose,
like the man's, was narrow and angular, sloping precariously to
the groove above his upper lip. I placed a finger in the groove
and felt the bursts of hot breath. I did not let the thought carry
me too far, aware—faintly—where it might lead me.

I turned to undress the man, taking off his work shirt and pants,
and pulled the bed cover over him. The man slept soundly—his
drilling snores had started up—and I was suddenly overwhelmed
by an inexplicable rush of rage, at the man's utter ignorance, at his
irreproachability, untouched by the knowledge that had already
sunk its roots inside me, gripping me tight, choking. How I had
wanted, there and then, to bring a fist to the things he held close,
to shatter them. How I wished to destroy everything he had or
believed or wanted—just to make him see—*see what you have done
to us, to the boy, to me. See what you have done with your own hands.*

Why was I angry with him? What did he do?

Everything. He wasted my life.

What do I mean?

I got to know the man at my first job, at an advertising agency
where I worked, fresh out of design school. I was working as a
junior copywriter and was new to everything: the people—the
hierarchy and pecking order—the office culture, the scope of my
job, my first stab at a professional work life. The man was an art
director then, on the rise, handling a few of the biggest accounts
for the agency. I, of course, had seen and heard about him before
I joined the company; he had come to my school in my final year
and given a talk—something about the sustainability of green
design in an eco-conscious age—at a design symposium held
for the graduating cohort, which I attended. He was disarmingly
charming and imposing on stage—traits he cultivated carefully and
used to his advantage when the occasion called for it. I recalled

being more impressed by his delivery, candid and engaging, than the contents of his talk. When the talk ended, I had hovered in the crowd convening around him, eager to catch a close-up of him, to take in his slick, polished handsomeness. *Isn't he the kind of guy who has everything,* one of my classmates, standing beside me, had said aloud. *Money, fame, career, a beautiful wife maybe, and lots of people who want to fuck him?*

On my first day at work, as I was taken around the office for introductions, the man had stepped out from behind his polished brass-and-oak desk and come right up to me to give me a firm handshake, a warm smile on his face. *Welcome to the family,* he had said, *you're a part of us now.* I smiled and looked down at my hands.

Before he left work that day, the man had stopped by my desk, a narrow cubicle tucked away in a dusty windowless corner of the office near a row of noisy photocopiers, and asked me about my first day. He waved briefly to dismiss the formality when I rose ungainly from my seat to acknowledge him. I knitted my fingers together behind me—to prevent them from fluttering too much, a sign of my nerves—and gave a short, truncated reply, choosing my words cautiously, not wanting to appear too flippant or ceremonious. He nodded as I spoke, then leant in and said: *I'm sure we would be working together very soon, and I can't wait.* He gave a wink, and left. In his wake, the air around me hung with the tart muskiness of his cologne.

And just like he said, we were soon working together on various projects and advertising campaigns, spending a good amount of time in each other's company. In person, the man was quick-witted, good-humoured, and adept at turning every situation into a funny or interesting anecdote or story. He never lacked the one thing that makes a man innately, irresistibly charming: a keen sense of self-confidence, and it was this very aspect of him that I was deeply drawn to. Perhaps it's the inherent attraction of what was missing in me, the pull of opposites. I was by nature shy and withdrawn, one who chose to stay away from anything that required me to make my presence known, preferring to stay on the sidelines, to be an observer rather than a participant, to listen rather than to speak. I was passive to the core, willing to stay in the shadow, compliant and unassertive. The man, having already read me through and through in our early days, took the effort to pry me open and to draw me out, first with his presence and later his guileful words.

It was a heady sensation, to be known by another person, to be seen so clearly without the need to hide. The man made it easy for me to fall in love with him, a helpless—hopeless—inevitability, given his subtle persistence and shrewdly calculated pursuit of me. He chose to make me the centre of his attention, and whenever I entered the meeting room or his office, he would cajole me with compliments and flattery, and keep a close proximity to me, within an arm's reach, whether he was standing or sitting beside me. The nimbus of his body heat, his mint-and-coffee breaths, the brush of his meaty fingers against mine. By the end of the second week, I was hanging on his every word, pathetically, like a dog on a leash, and tracking his movements around the office in my mind's eye, always eager and watchful and pining for his attention, the crumbs of his affection, alert to his every beck and call.

Given the roles and hierarchy in the agency, I had to report to him directly on specific projects we worked on, something that often caused me great anxiety, and also unabated elation. From the initial brief of a project—a one-to-one meeting with the man that often left me scribbling chicken-scrawls on my notepad, my entire focus fixed on the immediate reality of his body so close to mine—to the first draft of copy I wrote. Throughout the three-month probation period at work, I was made very aware of the man's unwavering scrutiny of me, an assiduous, purposeful effort to wedge himself into my consciousness, to secure my notice and regard. I was, of course, quick to respond in my clumsy, too-obvious ways, to his overtures. He was patient with the draft copies. He never raised a voice at my mistakes—though I had heard numerous stories, circulated around the office, of him cutting designers and other copywriters down to size for the smallest of errors—and took pains to suggest changes and improvements. Once or twice, I intentionally let slip a minor detail, just to prove my own intuition, and was secretly gratified to see him responding indulgently, with imperturbable patience and warmth.

Still, everything that happened at the beginning of our courtship—what exactly do you call such a relationship, without slipping into the moral and judgmental—seduction, adultery—or making it seem infantile—crush, infatuation—happened in private, a personal matter known only to him and me. He never made it a point or did anything to bring it to light, to make his feelings for me publicly known, and I was happy to go along with it. Deception is a two-way street, paved with ambiguous intentions, I later thought. I was only twenty-two, and I was in love, and everything, anything, felt possible.

At first, we would head out for lunch or coffee with other colleagues, and then it gradually, naturally, progressed to meals with just the two of us. I would decline offers from my colleagues to eat out or to buy back food, and instead wait at my desk for the man to come by and ask me out for lunch when the office was nearly deserted. He would make it casual, as if his requests were simply something by-the-way, innocuous, and I would pause—I often kept myself busy with work, even more so during lunch-time—for a few seconds, lifting my pencil meaningfully in the air, before agreeing to it. We would grab something simple, at the nearby hawker centre or food court—the man knew enough to keep things above board, to keep up appearances—and it often seemed to me that time spent during these lunches was always too short, and in no time at all we would have to make our way back to the office. And whenever we came within the vicinity of the office, he would hold back, draw out a crumpled pack of Marlboro menthols from his pocket and signal his intention to have a quick smoke in the alley between the shop houses where the agency was situated, and nod at me to go ahead. I'd walk into the cool environ of the lobby, my face and insides flushed with a diffident self-awareness.

Perhaps because of his position at work, and also his age— he was fifteen years older—I took all my cues on how to act, respond and behave from the man and allowed him to direct the flow of our conversations at work and over meals, letting him ask the questions while I gave my replies promptly and directly, and occasionally ventured a question or two, though nothing personal or probing. It would have been highly inappropriate for me to be direct and forthcoming, even though I was extremely curious about the man, his thoughts, his life outside of work. What was he like in a different place, in a different role, doing something else: cooking himself a meal, running in a park, talking to his parents, playing with a dog? How different would he be from the person that was right in front of me? How exactly was he living his life, away and apart from me, from our daily interactions? It was impossible, almost absurd, not to take a fervid interest in the man and all the things he did; I wanted to know everything about him. But in time, I reminded and assured myself, soon, soon.

We started having our lunch in restaurants farther away from the office, driving to the venue in his black BMW, but always making sure to come back on time. He would suggest these restaurants—his favourites, he claimed—small, intimate, dark-interior places with menu prices that were twice, sometimes thrice, the amount I had set aside for my monthly meals. I'd order a salad or a simple appetizer, citing a heavy breakfast, but the man would override my decision and order something from the mains for me, going into raptures about the artisan method of cooking that particular entrée or the unique and specific ingredients sourced from Finland or a hilly village on the island of Shikoku. The man would then pay for the meals and refuse all my entreaties to pay him back.

Back in the office, after our secret lunches, he would revert to his serious, officious self, maintaining a prim distance—and again, taking the cue from him, I would do likewise—and going about his work in the same cogent, orderly way. He never did break character, as if he were on a stage, performing before an audience, his lines and movements and mannerisms already internalized, smooth and natural, ingrained. Method acting, I thought, only the best performers could do this, to slip so fully and immerse themselves into another character. Daniel Day-Lewis, Christian Bale, Joaquin Phoenix. And then the man. Watching him was like watching a man with many surfaces, catching different lights, shiny and bright and all too entrancing; I would not look away, even if I could. He drew in everything, a black hole that devoured all, light and matter.

But could I? Maybe it's easier to say I didn't want to look away.

I was in love with him. I love him.

This is not love? But something else?

What?

It's love.

I don't know what I'm talking about?

He's the first man I loved. He's my first love.

I love him.

It's really love.

I don't have to convince you or anyone else.

Yes, it is.

There were, of course, stories and gossips floating around the office about the man, and while I had heard them all—I sought these stories out, discreetly, like a person gathering pieces of a scattered puzzle—I was selective about which ones to believe, and which to ignore. That he was a womanizer was common knowledge, an open secret—two account-servicing executives from his former workplace had allegedly quit on account of his serial philandering, one after the other, barely three months apart—though it had not put me off at the time, perhaps out of naivety and, I think, more out of inane vanity, for I was flattered by the man's constant attention on me. I was the one, the only one he wanted. It had been widely speculated that he was seeing someone—not me, but a senior designer, apparently—from the office and was keeping the affair a secret, but after a fortnight of close observation, I could find nothing to justify the rumour— perhaps, because the designer in question was a sad, dumpy woman in her early thirties, with a bad case of body odour and an even worse dress sense, circulating her wardrobe of bright, gaudy sweaters and huge floral dresses. I could not imagine the man finding anything desirable in such a woman. What could the woman have that I did not already possess in spades: youth, docility, discretion. As for the other things that were said about the man—his family, his spoilt lavish lifestyle, his impending balding—I remained disinterested, refusing to let them affect me. Who was without faults or flaws, I thought, who would cast the first stone?

Am I always so good at deceiving myself? To hear what I want to hear, and to hell with everything else?

Maybe. Don't we all?

Then why did he lie to me?

He didn't, not at first. He was very upfront about what he wanted me to know, about what was at stake.

Yes, I believed him.

For some time, we kept what went on between us under cover, cautious about drawing unnecessary attention to ourselves. On the surface, I continued to play my role as a hardworking, diligent subordinate and fellow colleague, discharging my duties and meeting deadlines, staying late when there was a need, and putting in good time to complete an urgent task or project when I was called to. I was conscientious, unflappable, someone with a deep purpose, with staunch conviction. Inwardly I could feel myself growing and extending the limits of who I was, becoming a woman who was capable of love and also capable of bending herself to the demands of that love. I opened myself to everything the man gave—and he was generous in the giving—and in return, I offered what I could give freely, without restraint: my devotion, perfect and undivided.

We spent more and more time together, out of the office, in our free time: catching a movie on weekends, checking out a new restaurant or café, visiting museums, even heading out of town on two- or three-day trips, to Bangkok, Langkawi, and Bali. He paid for everything and took care of all arrangements. He never once allowed me to lift a finger in any of the planning, preferring to take charge of all the details, keeping me in the dark till he sprang the surprise. *Why are you so good to me*, I said, on more than one occasion, to which the man often replied: *Because I want to.*

On the first night of our first overseas trip to Kuala Lumpur, lying on the sweat-soaked bed, the man had turned to me and said: *You know what all this means, right? You know what's involved, what you needed to do. I need to be sure you know this.*

I folded my arms around him, drawing him tighter into my embrace, and replied: *Yes, I know, I understand.*

For my compliance and silence, the man was unsparing in his efforts to secure my love, to make me his. In my first year on the job, I was chosen to work on several prominent advertising campaigns for some of the agency's blue-chip clients—the man made sure to bring me on board projects that were the most visible and important, not by direct appointment, which would smack openly of favouritism, but by subtle persuasion, to the other team leads. In all, I was given much opportunity to develop my abilities, with him guiding me along the way. In that same year, I was promoted to senior copywriter with a decent pay raise, much to the surprise of the other new hires; the man had put in a good word for me at the annual appraisal. I kept my head low, my demeanour humbled, politely shrugging off congratulatory praises from the other colleagues, buying them a round of lemon tarts and bubble teas to thank them for their help and support. With my newly adjusted pay, I shopped and bought the man a pair of Tiffany cufflinks, in sterling steel and shaped in the symbols of hugs and kisses, which he took to wearing the day after I gave him, though he had chided me lightly for wasting money, that he did not need anything from me.

No, I didn't allow myself to be used by him.

He did all these things for me because he loves me.

Was I silly? Too dumb for my own good?

You said he had a point to prove?

That he could have me at his beck and call? That I would come crawling to him whenever he wanted me to?

He isn't always a selfish bastard.

No, you're missing the whole picture.

Am I?

If there was one person who was selfish in the relationship, it was me, undoubtedly, hard to admit as it was. I was the one who wanted more—of his time, of his attention, of his love. I watched him closely as he moved around the office, unable to pull my gaze away, observing how he interacted with the other women, how he commented on their outfits and looks, flirting

with them with his honeyed words, how he leant into them
sometimes to whisper words into their ears, laughing along with
them. I pretended not to mind—he was only putting on a show,
to divert the attention away from what was really going on, he
told me once. *You won't believe how much people like to talk about
themselves all the time, given any chance*, he said, *so just let them talk.*
It was all to pretend that he was interested in someone else,
while in truth his whole fixation, his unswerving devotion, was
on me, only me. I never looked away. I wanted to see how far
he would go, in his pretence, his ruses, even when I was there.
It had pained me to look, but the price of not looking was
something I could not afford.

I like to do that, don't I? To inflict pain on myself, for no
good reason.

It's hard to change. I'm a masochist at heart, perhaps.

Go ahead, laugh all you want.

No, some pain is always good. It keeps you alive, makes you
feel real.

You ought to know that.

So, while the man was open about who he was and what
he was doing for us, he was very careful to keep certain things
in the dark, to leave them out of our conversations. He never
talked about his family, for one, and any curiosity on my part
was quickly brushed aside or ignored. The bits of stories I sought
from the other colleagues, those who had worked with the man
longer than I did, were few and far between, and did nothing to
quell the questions in my head. A few times, while we were out
for lunch or on a date, the man would receive a call or text on his
mobile and pull brusquely away from me, putting his finger to
his lips—a sign for me to keep mum—and begin to whisper into
it, his head bent low in stern concentration. Sometimes, within
earshot, I would catch a word or two from these conversations,

but whatever meaning they conveyed was lost to me—there was very little to piece everything together, this not insignificant part of the man's life that was lost or hidden from me.

When he came back to me, he would dismiss these calls as nuisance, a chore, not elaborating further. I might have believed him, if not for the darkening of his features that took a while to dispel. Once, his mobile had vibrated during a team discussion in the office and, sitting beside him, I had peeked at the caller's name flashing on the screen and quickly looked away, barely able to suppress my annoyance. When I asked the man later, privately, about this, he had turned to me, his face tightened into an ugly scowl, and said: *You already knew what was involved, didn't you? Don't act like you didn't know.*

I tamped down the rage simmering inside me and said nothing. While the issue continued to eat at me afterwards, I did not bring it up again.

Still, like a missing tooth in one's mouth, I kept prodding at the hole and rimming the bloody edges. I soon learnt to pay attention to what was left out of our conversations and to look out for omissions in the silences; I listened, like a hunter listened in the forest: poised, vigilant, attuned to every sound, yet discerning enough to make out the specific footfall of a prey. I even went to the extent of recording our conversations on my phone, before and after our sessions in the hotels, and listened to them over and over again, not only for what the man had said and promised—and there were so many promises—but also for the things that I might have missed out at the time, in the rush to hear only the things I wanted to hear. Occasionally I would transcribe some of the more important conversations, noting down the crucial or illuminating details in my journal, accumulating them like an animal storing up food for a long hibernation. Then I would delete the recordings from my phone.

Yet, even after doing all this, it felt insufficient, inadequate, as if the more I heard, and the man could talk a blue streak, the wider the chasm grew between us. So many words, mounting up over time. And what did they amount to, what had they revealed? An ever-increasing canvas whose outline and many details, upon closer inspection, were nothing more than smudges and smears, bleeding and blurring into one another. The supposed clarity was only, simply, an illusion, held together by distance and perspective.

One time, while he was in the shower, I had taken his wallet out of his trouser pocket, peeped at his IC and written down his home address. When he could not meet me one weekend, giving the excuse of a dental appointment, I had taken a taxi down to his place, a huge bungalow along Thomson Road, with a large courtyard in the front. Standing on the opposite side of the road, hiding myself partially behind a parked Volvo, I stared at the house, trying to peek into his other life—with his wife and child.

Through the white-lace curtains of the living room, I could make out vague silhouettes of people moving and sitting and standing inside, though I was not able to tell them apart. I recalled a dog, though I did not see it, only heard its barks coming from somewhere inside the house. I waited to catch a glimpse of the man, but he did not appear. I have forgotten how long I had stayed that first time, but when I saw someone parting the curtains and looking out, I panicked and quickly walked away, my whole body whirring with dread and electricity.

And, yet, I returned for another visit, not long after that, and then another; the visits were something I did without thinking too much or weighing the consequences. If I had, I might have reasoned myself out of them. I just couldn't stop. The risks were no longer something I considered. And with each visit, whether it was only ten minutes or an hour, I would take away something from it: a glimpse of the man, his still slim, still beautiful wife, the laughter of his young daughter, their going about their day, their chores, eating together, watching TV, singing karaoke, hanging out with their friends, whose bulky BMWs and Audis and Lexus filled the long driveway and out onto the road, parked bumper to bumper. The meaty smell of the barbeque, the boisterous chorus of children's shouts and cheers, the loud percussive music seeping out into the air, overlaying the heated racket. Once, I had stayed till the man went around the house, turning off the lights, one by one, the interior falling into darkness. The master bedroom, right at the top of the bungalow, the fortress, from where the amber light filtered dimly through the curtained windows was the last to be snuffed out. Did he kiss his wife before he turned in every night, I often wondered, did he fuck her till they both come before sinking into sleep, nestled in each other's arms? Did he lay out glasses of water on the tables on both sides of the bed, taking two sips of his before shutting his eyes, as he always did when he was with me? Did he snore or fart or murmur or cry out in his sleep? Did he ever surface from his dream, hard and yearning, dreaming of me, craving for my breasts, my cunt, my open, willing mouth? Did he ever wonder where I was, what I was thinking, what I was doing? Did he have any idea who I was?

If the man knew about these visits, he would have been appalled, even enraged.

You saw me? A couple of times? Really?

Well, I saw you too. What a beautiful girl, I remembered telling myself, the first time I saw you with the man.

Don't blush, it's true.

Don't look away.

Come, take my hand. Is it cold? I need to know you're still here.

Why are you hiding your face from me? Why won't you let me see you now?

Yes, you can ask me anything.

Why didn't I tell the man about the boy?

I wanted to, but by then it's too late.

I didn't lie to him.

The man spent the night at the house and left very early in the morning, without breakfast. I was awake long before him; in fact, I did not sleep at all. I got out of bed after some time, thinking about the boy in his bedroom under the thick blanket. On several occasions, I thought I heard noises coming from his room; perhaps the boy had finally come to and was calling out for me, needing me. The house was playing tricks on me, mocking and taunting me. Still I went and stood outside the boy's bedroom, listening in, hearing nothing. I checked the door; it was locked. I walked around the house and finally lay down on the sofa in the living room, staring out the glass windows at the mango tree in the garden. The sight of it was an odd balm to my tired, wary mind, displacing my restless thoughts with images of ripe mangoes hanging heavily from the dark branches, my mind crawling through the network of the tree's limbs and hands, higher and deeper into its canopy. Whenever I closed my eyes my mind would congeal into a blank. I passed the long hours of the night with nothing to break the surface of this blankness, as if I were suspended in a sack of dead air at the bottom of an ocean. When I heard a sharp knock coming from upstairs—was the boy awake in his room?—I stumbled clumsily out of the sofa and banged my shin against the blunt edge of the coffee table, the sharp pain wrenching me right out of the illusion, my fantasy. *Stop it, get over yourself, it's no use thinking of this now*, I berated myself, in a hoarse voice entirely unlike my own. After a long moment of putting my thoughts in order, I eventually got up and went to prepare breakfast. I set the coffee machine to work with a fresh brew and took out the carton of skim milk and kaya spread from the fridge. The sky outside the windows was a sea of muted blues, the night slowly loosening its hold.

I was barely done with the toast—warm and crusty in my hands; everything seemed to take on new significance that morning—when the man burst into the kitchen, reeking of fresh cologne, mouthed a quick word about a presentation he needed to finish up for a client meeting later, and left with a kiss on my cheek. I wished the man a good day, summoning up a benevolent smile. From a side window, I saw him reverse the BMW out of the house and give me a wave, before driving off with a deep-throated rumble. I threw away the toast and poured away the coffee—when was the last time I ate? I could not remember—and started washing up the plate and cup and butter knife.

After that, I went about cleaning the whole house.

The boy? He's still in the room.

I'm not beating around the bush. I'm not stalling for time. I didn't do anything to him.

Yes, I did nothing, I left him alone in the room.

No, I didn't go into his room that day.

For a few days.

'Cause I was still deciding what to do then. I needed time to think.

Why do you always say I'm not telling the truth? Why made you think I'm lying to you? Why would I?

No, I'm not.

He's dead, where else could he go?

No, I don't expect you to believe this, if you don't want to.

I don't care what you believe.

Why do I need to lie to you?

No, I'm telling you everything I did.

No, I'm not making things up.

Up to you whether you believe me or not.

Did the man find out later?

No, I never told him.

Yes, I kept it from him.

He doesn't need to know.

Why?

Because of what he has done. He doesn't deserve to know.

What did he do?

Let me think. Don't rush me.

I can't keep talking, my throat is so dry, and the pain in my head, it's killing me. I can't think properly, I can't keep my thoughts straight.

Just stop talking, please. Can I have some silence, please?

Okay.

Just let me close my eyes for a while.

What do I see?

You. The man. The boy.

Where?

Let me think.

Maybe I should tell you a new story.

Yes, it's important. You'll understand when I'm done with it.

Listen.

I had always wanted a different life since I was young. I was an only child, my mother a seamstress, my father absent for so long—he left us for another woman, started another family and had three other children—that I could barely remember how he looked. I really didn't care to recall anything about him. There was hardly anything worth remembering about him in any case: a pair of callused hand, a head of wiry grey hair, a voice raspy from smoking. He was there one day, and then he wasn't, his stark absence standing in for the void. I might have cried over his disappearance, I don't know, but the seasons quickly passed and

I soon got over it. His abandonment became the elephant in the room neither my mother nor I wanted to address, skirting it as we swiftly, stubbornly, resumed our disrupted lives. My mother and I lived with the little we had. Her income barely covered the basic necessities but we managed to scrape by somehow, she with her small loans from our relatives from time to time, and I with my unfussy, undemanding nature, having learnt to live with just the bare essentials.

Because of my mother's job, the tiny one-room flat we lived in was constantly filled from wall to wall with carton boxes of dismembered sleeves and collars and strips of fabric, barely leaving us enough room for a small folding table for our meals and two thin mattresses for us to sleep on. My mother would be at her Singer sewing machine—a black glistening contraption, muscular with curves and solid lines, in my child's eye, bought by my father in instalments—the only good and useful thing he left her. Her hand would be on the balance wheel, turning and turning, first thing in the morning, before I was even awake, only pausing to make me breakfast and send me off to school.

Some mornings, lying very still on the mattress after I woke, my eyes gummy with sticky sleep, I would turn to study her foot on the pedal, the shapely protuberance of her thin ankle, tapping in time to a synchronized rhythm, and be lulled back into a hushed dream-state, not wanting the spell to be broken. The metallic clicks of the pedal as it went up and down, beating out a regular cadence that I timed with my breaths, in and out, my eyes getting heavier by the second, dropping off into snatches of sleep. Her voice, when she looked up at the clock on the wall and realized the time, would break through my daze, and I would reluctantly crawl out of the mattress, fold it up, plop it against the wall, and prepare for school.

When I returned from school in the afternoon, my mother would still be at the sewing machine, head bent low, a few boxes already sealed beside her, part of her daily consignment done. My mother was methodical and meticulous in how she kept the flat in order, ensuring that there was a proper sequence to how things were arranged and stored, with the newest assignment of boxes stacked near the kitchen while the ones she had completed piled beside the front door, waiting for the pick-up by the contractor who had hired my mother for the sewing job. Upon receiving a new batch, she would mark the delivery and collection dates on them. The carton boxes, and sometimes huge plastic carrier bags, were brought in weekly by a bald, plump man with red scaly hands and a slight lisp, whom I'd avoid studiously after a perfunctory greeting—my mother had insisted that I greeted everyone with an 'uncle' or 'auntie', whether or not I knew them or liked them, constantly reminding me that she didn't raise me to be a rude, ill-bred child. But in this case, I did not want to bear with the bald man's persistent pawing, his hand on my head and down my back, pinching my cheeks. Sometimes he would coax me with a treat of White Rabbit candies or a box of Ding Dang milk chocolate, which I'd grab out of his hand before he could reach out to touch me. *What a pretty girl you got there*, the man would say to my mother, who would give him a thin, hollow smile, before returning to their earlier conversation, ignoring me completely.

After the man left, my mother would task me to follow the order that she had set up and put me to work on arranging the boxes into their proper places, along with a thorough sweeping of the flat, to clean up the clumps of loose threads and discarded strips of fabric. Some days, she would have me sweep the floor three or four times if she spotted a single thread lying around during her inspection. Cleanliness was my mother's abiding virtue, her ceaseless fixation. She hated mess of any kind and was always ready with a quick word or slap if I made one—till this day, I drop everything to clear up a mess, an impulse that has become second nature to me.

Every day, before she put the black plastic cover over the Singer, she would tidy up the needles and buttons and spools of thread, returning them back to their respective slots in the sewing machine, and run a rag over the exposed surfaces, avoiding the moving metal parts, which she would grease generously with a can of WD-40 thrice a week. She took utmost care of the Singer, as if it were a living object that required her constant attention, the third member of our pitiable family.

After our dinner—usually rice and one or two vegetables dishes, rarely any meats, which were reserved solely for important festive dates on the lunar calendar, like the birthdays of deities— my mother would take her sewing kit out from a woven basket, and begin working on the odd sewing jobs she had picked up from a small pool of clients, mostly neighbours who needed to fix a torn sleeve or lengthen a pair of shorts or work pants. I would stay by her side, either doing my homework or reading— my mother had refused to buy a television, full of rubbish and nonsense, she said—sometimes sneaking glances at her, watching how her fingers would move deftly across the fabric, bringing all the different pieces together, pulling the thread to the farthest reach, tugging it a few times, and then severing it with a quick tear of her teeth. She took her time with these sewing jobs, never hurrying, ensuring everything was done right according to requests and specifications; she knew about quality of work, and the word-of-mouth publicity that could come out of it, which would determine whether we had enough to last the month or the next. She never turned down any job, no matter how badly they paid, and even as a child, I knew instinctively how miserly some of our neighbours were, bargaining with my mother, paying less for what was agreed upon, pressing a small handful of coins into her hand, brushing off her entreaties. Still, when the same neighbours came around the next time, my mother would take in their requests, submissive to their bidding. *Every cent earned is a cent in our pockets*, my mother reminded me, putting aside the small sums of money in a beaded coin purse tucked in the bottom drawer of the cupboard. Once, in a gush of childish pride, I told my mother I wanted to be a seamstress like her, to learn how to sew, and she gave me a blistering look, and said: *No, you'll not be like me. I didn't work so hard for you to be like me.*

After that, my mother refused to let me come near the sewing machine, let alone touch a needle, always pushing me back to my textbooks, my school assignments. Whenever I peeked at her during the breaks in my studies, I would catch a peculiar look on her face, if she happened to notice my glance, one that seemed to say: *No, not like me.* She was determined to see me become a different woman, one better and more capable in her eyes, and live a life that wasn't like the one she had, with a failed marriage, her husband deserting the family. With her firm, restraining hands on me, I had no choice but to turn aside, against my own wishes and ambition, and become the woman she was not. I put all my efforts into my school work, ensuring good grades through my primary and secondary school, and later junior college.

No, I wasn't happy at all.

It wasn't the life I wanted.

Yes, I wanted a good job, a good salary, of course, who doesn't?

But then I met the man, and I fell in love with him, along the way. No, I'm not saying it's not good enough for me. And I'm not saying it's an excuse.

I don't know that.

I don't know whether things would have turned out differently if I had not met him.

Why?

It's hard to say. Don't we all fantasize about having a different life at some point? The life that could have been if we had taken a different path, made a different choice.

No, these imaginary lives don't matter. What mattered in the end is the life I had, then, now.

Why did I change?

You want to know what happened to make me change? Why I did what I did?

Did what?

Did the boy tell you that? Why did you believe him? Why did you choose to believe him?

Do you not understand a single thing I've told you so far? Why is it so hard for you to believe my story? To believe me?

Here I am, telling it as it is.

Lies, lies, lies, and not one word of truth?

I'm not sure what you want me to say.

I'm not sure what you want of me.

Listen, just listen.

My mother had a strong, forceful personality, despite her meek, outwardly docile front that she presented to others. Like the violent churning of currents under the placid surface of a river, her strength and steely will were invisible to the naked eye, manifested only in her actions towards me. She demanded absolute obedience from me at all times. She would set out what she wanted from me—from the grades I got to the time I spent studying at home, along with a fixed set of rules and expectations that governed every part of my life—and I would follow them without question. Maybe it was the way we lived, just the two of us, from the very beginning, and, because my mother had taken such a dogged, unassailable hold of our lives that I could not envision a single aspect of my existence without her direct influence or imprint, from how I dressed—she made all the clothes we wore, from the scrapes she saved from the sewing jobs, clothes that fitted my body perfectly, with their long pretty sleeves and knee-length hems and Peter Pan collars, snug like a second skin—to what I was eating. To save money, we hardly ever ate out and everything my mother cooked was either steamed or boiled, nothing deep-fried, which she found greasy and unhealthy. She held the helm of our lives, defining and determining the exact limit and manner of how we should live. Everything had been decided for me, right from the start, for my benefit, nothing left to chance.

Any deviance or diversion in my behaviour was not tolerated and was dealt with swiftly with a lengthy caning, which happened only a few times in my childhood. I was never one to give my mother much grief for my conduct since the rare infractions I committed were done, not out of a perverse need to test the boundaries that had already been established firmly in place for me to obey and follow from a young age, but out of carelessness and ignorance, like a child discovering the burn of a paper cut only when the wound met water. I was a fast, avid learner—and I had learnt to read and interpret my mother's every action and word carefully, staunchly, like a loyal, watchful subject attuned to the changing moods of the monarch—and was quick not to repeat any mistake, to always toe the line. I did everything, not because I wanted to avoid the scoldings and punishments but out of a greater need to please my mother, to shape my love and devotion into the precise form and in the exact way she wanted it. All I had to do was simply listen, obey and submit— nothing more was asked of me. After all, all I wanted, in the end, was to be loved by her. But the love my mother had demanded of me was an immense, all-consuming one, one that took up everything in my life.

And when the man came into my life later, he became that everything, my all in all, after my mother died.

What happened to my mother?

She died.

Of what?

She committed suicide. Jumped from the flat. I saw her jump.

Why didn't I stop her?

I did, I tried, but she had stopped listening to me.

She was depressed, had been for a long time.

Yes, I should have known. I could have helped.

No, she didn't seek any help, not that I knew of.

From who, you tell me? It'd have been unthinkable. She was from a generation that didn't believe in such things, or even acknowledge the fact that she was suffering from it. It could have been so many other things.

Did I know she was suffering from depression?

Perhaps I did know, somehow.

I lived with her my whole life. I saw everything she didn't want to see or couldn't possibly understand. She was a deeply unhappy woman.

No, unhappiness is not depression.

Maybe I was wrong.

But I was there, I know what I saw. I saw how she was, what she did, what she couldn't help doing.

No, I did help her. I didn't just leave her alone.

I tried. I did. But by then she was beyond help.

My mother had always tried her best to keep things—her insecurities, her unexpressed fears, her weaknesses—from me, but given the close proximity of our entwined lives, it was hard, almost impossible, to keep a tight lid on her own moods, which could change in a split second, many times over a single day. Her rage, when it came and it could come swiftly, unpredictably, was reckless and formidable, sweeping a clean path through any reason or explanation. Once, I was half an hour late coming back from school—I was in secondary school then—she had poured out the contents of my school bag to check for cigarettes—*Why are you stinking of smoke? I can smell it off you!*—and ordered me to strip off my school uniform and wash it at the kitchen sink with a brush and soap. No matter how hard I tried to defend myself, to deny her false accusation, my pleas all but fell on deaf ears. And for a week after that, she would wait at the school gates for my classes to end, just so she could keep a close eye on me, her presence beside me a shaming reminder of her deep distrust.

At my age then, twelve going on thirteen, my mother was constantly warning me to stay away from the boys in school, not to talk to them, and told me lurid stories, gleaned from the sordid headlines of the nightly Chinese newspapers, about new-born babies abandoned in public toilets or thrown down the rubbish chutes, and the increasing rate of sexually-transmitted diseases among teenagers. *You see, this is what can happen to you if you're not careful and let the boys have their way with you,* she would scream at me, thrusting the front page of the newspapers into my face, *is that what you want, you tell me, is it?*

The first time I had my period—I had woken in the morning to a sprawling dark-red stain on the mattress—I thought I had somehow cut myself during sleep, with the rusty zipper on the edge of the mattress. I dabbed at the stain with my fingers, the blood still damp, smelling of raw minerals. It was only seconds later, looking down at my pink Minnie Mouse shorts that I noticed, gasping with sharp alarm, a corresponding patch of blood on the crotch area, and was startled by the sight. What had I done—always the fear of the consequences of my actions, trailing in the wake of anything that happened to me, what had I done again, what did I do wrong—to cause this, to bleed like this? Later, when my mother saw the blood on my shorts, she instructed me to look at that blotch of blood long and hard and gave me a scathing lecture about what it was—*the filthy blood purged from your body, you'll have it every month*—and what it meant—*you'll get pregnant if you let a boy stick his thing into you.* Whatever fear or anxiety I had felt at seeing my own menstrual blood quickly gave way to a crippling, maddening sense of humiliation. Washing my stained pyjamas at the kitchen sink, with my mother supervising and watching behind my back, I could not keep my hands from trembling or my thoughts from wheeling. The incipient knowledge of what my body was capable of spread darkly through every inch of my flesh, like a portentous sign, a heavy burden. Under the running water, the dried blood from the shorts ran from red to pink, getting under my fingernails. The stain eventually came off after several thorough rinses, with a dab of baking soda, leaving behind a very faint brown outline. My mother refused to let me hang it outside on the bamboo poles with the rest of our regular laundry, telling me to put it out of sight, in the bathroom. I didn't wear those shorts again, hiding it in a bag of old clothes at the back of the cupboard.

That morning, after I took a long shower to wash off any residual blood—I was wary of touching myself, though I was told to wash it clean, and ran my hand roughly down the tight pouch of my crotch, rubbing it a few times with the cold water gushing from the rubber hose affixed to the tap, my forefinger furtively tracing the thick line of my slit, the whole act releasing a wave of conflicting sensations that rippled from the core of my body to its extremities, a tantalizing shiver of guilt and shame—my mother handed me a strip of white cloth—a rag, really—and told me to *stuff it down there*. I did as I was told, and I was so self-conscious the whole time I was in school that I refused to leave my seat or go for my break during recess, afraid that any vigorous movement on my part would cause me to bleed anew. Looking around at the other girls in my class, those already wearing bras with the straps showing through their white translucent tops, I wondered whether they too had undergone the same sort of experience, whether they had been surprised, mortified, by their first period.

Later, coming back from school, my mother handed me a box of sanitary napkins, telling me to read the instructions on the back of it. I exchanged the rag, streaked generously with blood, for a sanitary pad, adjusting the latter to find a comfortable fit, and throwing the former into a plastic bag, provided by my mother, which I then discarded down the rubbish chute. *No one needs to see how much you have bled*, my mother had warned, *it's disgusting*.

For a long time after the incident, I was extremely wary of my own body, watching it as if it were something that could trip me up, or worse, betray me, at any time with little or no provocation. Using the calendar on the back of a school-issued diary, I started crossing off the days from one period to another, counting down, making sure I was prepared for it. The actual period might be off a day or two, but I was never again surprised by its occurrence, always carrying extra sanitary napkins in a dark-blue drawstring bag that I stuffed deep into my school bag, just in case. In the span of a few months, my breasts began to swell, contouring the front of my shirt, and dark wiry strands of hair sprouted first on my crotch, then in my armpits. I tried to cut off this newly grown hair with a pair of stationery scissors, but that only caused them to proliferate faster, thickening in texture. I grew acutely aware of how I smelled when I perspired, detecting a stronger, gamier pungency to my sweat, which I tried to mask with scented wet wipes throughout the day. Everything seemed to be in flux—the permanent, irreversible changes taking place in my body, racing ahead of me, leaving me stranded, trapped in a child's mind. I was a stranger, a foreigner, living in my own body, observing it from a distance, viewing it as if through the lens of a microscope, which magnified and distorted all that I saw in myself. My body, I came to realize, was something that had to be monitored, to be scrutinized at every turn, lest it grew unmanageable, mutinous.

My mother, already way ahead of me when it came to this, bought me five thick beige-coloured bras and matching panties shortly after my first period, which I duly wore, like pieces of a new costume, uncomfortable and awkward on my changing body, pinching and chafing my skin with its edges and fit. I changed them daily, washing them separately by hand, hanging them to dry inside the flat, embarrassed by the sight of them. When I was out with my mother, on errands and grocery runs, I'd notice my mother's censorious gaze on me, inspecting my every move and gesture. *Don't sit like that, don't talk so loud, don't slouch, don't point, don't stare*, my mother would say, slapping the offending part of my body into submission. Whenever she caught someone, a man, looking at me, she would lean in and snap at me, *don't flaunt, don't walk with your legs so wide, don't draw attention to yourself, don't be a little slut*. Having her beside me was like having a spotlight trained on me constantly, never missing any of my slips, my mistakes, never once letting up.

It was not hard, thinking back, to understand the motives behind my mother's actions, her manic protectiveness over me—she had married young, at nineteen, and later became a single mother when I was barely five. She had not considered the support of her own family who had disowned her when she chose to marry my father, a low-wage worker in a textile factory, who subsequently abandoned her for another woman. In her sporadic and increasingly harsh tirades over the years of my adolescence, mostly directed at me—and perhaps, in some covert way, at herself, too—my mother would bemoan her fate and terrible life and all the injustices she had to suffer for my sake. *If only I'd thrown you down the flat when you're a baby or smothered you in your sleep, if only I'd the courage, I could have a different life, a better one than this*, she would lash out, specks of spittle flying out of her mouth.

Whenever she went into one of these episodes, which would occasionally progress into rounds of slaps and punches aimed at me, I'd hunch my body, keeping it small and tight, wrapping my arms around my head, and wait for her wrath to pass over like a terrible storm subsiding. They didn't last long, these beatings, a few minutes tops, before my mother's rage started to flag, her strength sapping, her words losing their venom and intensity. It had never crossed my mind to put up a fight or to retaliate, not once; I had always assumed it was me, or something in me, a clear and undeniable flaw, that drew out this madness from my mother. It hurt, naturally, what she dealt out to me, but I knew it was my dues, for who I was, deep inside.

No, I never once retaliated.

What was the point? It'd only make her angrier.

No, I didn't tell anyone about these beatings.

Who could I possibly tell it to?

Why? What could they do? What would they know?

I didn't need any help.

My mother, when she broke from these fevers of madness, would become chastened, extremely remorseful, overcompensating with overt displays of indulgence and affection. She would hold me tight to her chest, her tears falling into my hair, onto my face, coursing alongside mine, rocking our bodies side to side, whipping herself up into a state of penitence. After she had calmed down sufficiently, she would immediately take to rubbing medicinal ointments on my bruises and applying iodine and plasters to the cuts, cooing soft apologies to me, waiting for my responses. *See what you made me do*, she would say, *why don't you listen to me, why do you always let me get so mad at you.* I'd nod dutifully and, in return, demonstrate my contrition by yielding to her ministrations without even a whimper, assuring her that it's okay, that I was okay, that I was sorry, that it wouldn't happen again. She would pat my head and smile benevolently down at me, her face lit with tenderness and kindness.

We would keep up a temporary truce until her next flare-up, which could happen several hours later, or in the next few days. It did not matter what the trigger was—over the careless mistakes in my Chinese homework, a phone call I received from a classmate, the length of my school skirt, the tone of my voice when I spoke with her—my mother would turn at the drop of a hat, coming fully at me with her sudden outbursts. I grew familiar with the little signs that preceded these fits—the narrowing of her eyes, the gradual rising of her arms, the speed at which she talked, her words gradually becoming incoherent—and would prepare myself to face what was coming, to endure what was inevitable. I could bear with anything when the time came, when I knew what was to be expected. Nothing surprised me by then. And in any case, I already had my strategy, I knew how to escape—through that voice in my head. The voice made it easier to bear with anything, with any pain.

Still, to paint my own mother in such harsh light was to do her a great injustice, to offer only one facet of who she really was, her true and complicated self, someone who loved me unfailingly, unconditionally. My mother went to great lengths to ensure that I had a good education and never held back on spending what I needed for my studies: enrichment classes, tuition for all my subjects, a brand-new laptop. With her eyes always on me, she was able to read and anticipate my every move, every word, with a startling exactitude, and respond appropriately, accordingly, with a rebuke, a rebuttal, an assent, a reward. With the close, symbiotic relationship we had, I, too, learnt to emulate and reciprocate, not only in how I related and responded to my mother, but also, by extension, in how I perceived and understood the people around me, how they acted and behaved towards me, how I should react to or requite their actions. It was a matter of survival, measured deliberation and discernment over pure instincts. To learn to see and grasp and anticipate someone else's next move, to be a step ahead—this was, I felt, my mother's greatest gift to me, something I could use—and often did—to get what I wanted.

Why is it a gift? Why is it important to me?

'Cause it's the only thing of real value that my mother left me after she died. And, because with it, I could anticipate what other people want from me.

What do they want from me?

What do I get in return?

Do I always get what I want?

No, not always, sometimes.

I don't need a lot of things.

For a long time, in the seamless years of my adolescence, I had lacked for nothing. There wasn't much I particularly wanted or desired. What my mother had provided in my life was enough for me then; she had taught me to live with less, to expect nothing to come easy, especially money. While my classmates were always clamouring for the next new thing—the latest iPhone, a Prada wallet, the most popular Korean nail-art manicure—I was happy to do without. *Possessions are addictions*, my mother used to say, as we walked past a shop or window display on our way to the wet market for our weekly groceries, *they tie you up, hold you down, they kill you in the end. They'll kill us?* I said. *Yes, your need to possess, to own things, they become your obsessions, they're the things that kill you*, my mother would repeat, jabbing a finger into my chest for emphasis. I would look at whatever was displayed before me—a pink knee-length dress on the battered mannequin, a pair of Gucci sunglasses—and think about how these things could possibly be associated with death. How would they become obsessions, I wondered, these bright, colourful things? What dangers could they pose to us? Death—was it possible? Do we court our own deaths with the things we crave? Do our desires slaughter us in the end? I spun these thoughts nonstop in my head—the pressure of my mother's finger on my chest, tapping, tapping—and gradually the pall of death fell like long drapes of shadow on the things I saw around me, things that could possess or even kill us—no, me.

Arriving at this realization, I decided there and then not to want anything—to desire nothing, in other words—and to stay far away from any ownership of things, the need to keep wanting, and wanting more. I had the same canvas sling bag and pencil case from primary to secondary school, not bothering to change them even when the trend for haversacks and large stationery pouches came into fashion, or when they became tattered and worn. Unlike my classmates who stuffed their bulging pouches with all sorts of coloured pens, highlighters and a dizzying assortment of Post-it stickers, I kept a small hoard of stationery, one of each essential: a blue Pilot pen, a Zebra mechanical pencil, an eraser, a Pentel correction tape, a yellow highlighter, a ruler, a stapler, a box of staples. I resisted the need to add to what I already had, replacing them when the ink ran dry or the tape or staples were used up. I had two hair clips, a set of black hair ties and a maroon scrunchie that I wore on a rotational basis—these were the furthest extent of my vanity. As for clothes, they were all made and tailored by my mother, except for my school uniform, which she took to adjusting the hem so the blue skirt came just below my knees; I don't think I owned a proper pair of jeans or pants or t-shirt till after my college. If there was a tear in any of my clothes, my mother would mend it; if something became too small for me, she would rip it up and use the pieces as rags, nothing gone to waste. During my mother's violent outbursts, she would occasionally slash a favourite shirt of mine or a childhood soft toy—I had four: Rex a red diplodocus, a Doraemon, a Mr Bean's teddy bear, and a mermaid with fraying plastic tail, birthday presents from my mother over the years, all of which I lost in the same year, a few months apart—with a pair of kitchen scissors and throw it down the rubbish chute. The initial loss was unbearable, but just as quickly, in all things relating to my mother, I learnt to master my own emotions, to mask my feelings behind a stony, unruffled face. I would not let it affect me, I told myself, tamping down the hurt and pain inside—they're nothing to me, they're useless, worthless possessions. And it was just as well, these early losses: they trained my heart to be tougher, more resilient, not to be too sentimental. What was the use of having things that could be so easily taken, to be destroyed, what real value did they have, what did they really mean to me?

All this was, of course, a child's callow thought—naïve, silly, untested. There are just so many things in the world that can ensnare us, that can kill us, and they're not always visible or apparent, things we can perceive with our bare eyes, that we can reject and say no to. It takes little to spurn what we had not wanted in the first place, what we could not have; it's much harder to dismiss the things that are within our grasp, that we know we could have, if only we do this or that, try a little harder, put in more effort, endure a bit longer: recognition, status, position, success, love. Intangible, incorporeal, unperishable as long as you hold these in our mind, whims and hopes made real, made possible, by our yearning. Not things that turn to dust or fade under the sun, that serve only fleeting needs, but things of a higher, greater nature, promising and offering something more, something lasting. Love, especially, that's our highest call, our deepest longing. We seek to possess what we love, who we love, to protect it, to guard it. People, relationships, family: it is our loves that possess us in the end, that kill us all. My love for my mother, for the man, for the boy.

It isn't love that I have for them?

How would you know?

I didn't do anything to them. No, I don't have to take a good look inside me to know that it's love.

Why don't you believe me?

Yes, but then, how do you separate love from possession?

No, no, I'm sure they love me, too.

I didn't have to make them love me. I didn't create the
illusion of love.

No, that's not true, you're wrong.

Stop, stop your nonsense.

Wait, do you smell it? That thick, awful smell, like a rotting
animal. Can you smell it? Is someone else in the room? Who is
it? Tell me.

What is it?

No, I don't find the smell familiar.

No, I don't have to think harder.

How would I know what smell this is?

What about this stench?

It only smells of death.

What does death smell of?

When I was nine, I think, that's how old I was when I first
came across death, to truly see its face. I knew what death is, of
course, at that age, I had witnessed it all the time: how my mother
killed the cockroaches and lizards in the flat, their exploded bodies
and creamy innards streaking the outsole of a slipper, the flattened
carcasses of pigeons and mynahs on the roads, by the curb, the
crushing of snails under my feet, fragments of shell melding with
the pulpy grey flesh. But these deaths were incidental, random,
and unforeseen. There was nothing to mark their differences.

I remember I was on my way to the neighbourhood library
after school ended that day. That was when I first encountered
it—the smell and the sight of the thing that had caused that
terrible smell—beside a tree in front of the library. At the base
of the tree, I saw a dead Calico cat with its belly ripped open
from neck to tail. Its body was propped against the tree, its limbs
splayed out, head drooping down to the chest. It would have
looked like a discarded soft toy, disembowelled of its stuffing,
if not for the dark greasy coils of innards hanging out of the

bloodied sack of its stomach, staining the soil around it nearly black. I had to blink a few times to make sure my mind was not playing tricks, that I had not imagined it. Both its eyes had been removed, leaving only dark empty holes. Perhaps it had died not long ago, I thought—or had it been dead for some time, I wasn't sure. No one thought to remove the mutilated body from the base of the tree, where it was laid out in a state of horrific repose. Had I been the first to discover it? Surely someone must have seen it, on the well-trodden path leading to the library, some kids, an adult, a concerned parent?

Whoever—and it only occurred to me much later, when I raked the memory up again, that someone must have butchered the cat, a real person or persons who had a hand in planning and executing this, this execution—had done it, had made a grand spectacle of the cat's death, to put it on display for everyone to see. I was too enthralled then, standing before death, drawn in by the sight of the dead cat, taking in every detail of its death, that I failed to make any logical connection, between the deed and perpetrator. The stench, as I walked up to the dead cat, was foul and aggressive, nearly physical, pushing its way into my nose. Fetid, yes, but also deeply organic, a dark smell pulled from some secret depth of the earth. I was not at all repulsed by it at the time.

Coming as close as I could, my feet touching the outermost edge of the blood stain on the dirt ground, I had leaned in to inspect the cat. A host of flies and ants was already making a feast in and around the emptied cavity of its soft belly, rallying all over the messy pale innards, bobbing like tiny quivering black beads, wet and glistening. I picked up a torn branch, broke it in two, and teased one of its splintered ends at the ragged flaps of the cat's stomach, lifting them and letting them fall dully against the body. I stuck the stick in as deep as it could go, moving it around gingerly, dislodging a trail of intestines hanging precariously at the edge of the flaps.

Getting bolder, I poked the bloodied stick into the empty eye-holes, and traced it delicately along the bony, gluey perimeter. I might have stayed there, at the tree, examining the body of the dead cat, for as long as I wanted—suspended in a sort of deep trance—if not for a sudden burst of anguished cry behind me, from a young girl, six, maybe seven, who had sneaked up quietly and seen the cat. Startled by her cry more than anything, I turned on my heel, threw the stick away and ran, inundated by a surge of conflicting dread and guilt, as if I had been personally involved in the cat's death.

It was really something to behold.

I've never seen anything quite like it before.

Death, laid out, in all its starkness and savagery, in plain sight.

Why do you think someone would do such a thing?

Why made such a public display of it?

Death, at a tree, near a library, for all to see.

Make of that what you will. It's really something, I tell you.

It reminded me, much later, in my second year in design school, when I was introduced to the art of Francis Bacon and I came across his piece, *Three Studies for a Crucifixion* that gave me quite a jolt. It was a triptych, and I was immediately struck by the central image of a pile of meat and bones, heaped on a seat, lumpy and bloody and contorted, twisted out of shape. It vaguely resembled a human body, if it was even that, minced and ravaged into such a state, destroyed. What is it, I thought, what am I seeing, this lump of flesh and colours? The longer I stared at it, into its bleeding interior, the deeper it pulled me into its gaping depth, where everything, the forms, parts, every shade of red, seemed to be swirling, twitching with life, growing with a force that came from nowhere—no, not nowhere, but from all that it's showing and exposing, forcing you to look, to really pay attention. What could be more fascinating, more shattering, than to see a creation of art that was like life itself, drawn from its very marrow? Life, art, death.

Do you know what I'm talking about? Do you understand?

Is it art, that dead cat at the tree?

No, I'm not laughing at you. It hurts to laugh.

Maybe, maybe.

What do I know about art at that age?

I only knew what I saw, and what I saw held me there, like a spell. It's impossible to turn or walk away from it. Something speaking to me, at me, calling out, something I felt deeply. Right here, in here.

Death is not something you can walk away from, just like that.

You just can't.

Of course, I had seen and witnessed other deaths after that, but never so close up and in such detail. That time, at the tree, I was beguiled by all the different intricate parts that made up a death—the flesh, the blood, and yes, the smell. It was such a heady mix—I could not get over the strong physical sensations it triggered, almost akin to an intoxication. The idea of death was no longer something abstract or remote, a thing quarantined from life, from my own life, but always around me, real, capricious, ever-present. It was something to take hold of, to savour, not push aside or ignore. Death is, after all, a part of life, its logical, unavoidable conclusion.

What about the boy?

What I did to him? What do you mean?

He drowned, he died. That was nothing I could do.

I couldn't save him.

All I could do for the boy was to clean him up, to wipe away the marks that death had left on him. As his mother, that's the least I could do for him. Three days after the man left for work and didn't come back home—he had returned to his bungalow, to his family, during this period—I finally entered the boy's room, peeled the blanket off his body and began my ministrations. His already-stiffened body was giving off a raw, rancid smell, slowly turning putrid. The gauze on his forehead was soaked through with blood, dark as grease. His face was a pale marble cast, preserving all his barren, lifeless features. Leaning into his chest and breathing in, I could catch faint whiffs of the boy's particular scent, rising, persisting weakly against the other complicit smells rising from his body. Not wanting to be drawn into the swamp of my thoughts, I quickly turned to my task. With a basin of water and a hand towel, I started scrubbing—an old memory suddenly surfaced: the long baths I had given the boy as a baby, lowering him into the warm sudsy water, rubbing a towel against his soft skin, the delicious peals of laughter that escaped his lips, his utter delight—and did not stop until the boy's body was rid of every visible sign of dirt and death, the water in the basin turning grey, silty. I laid the boy back on the bed, his skin clean and luminescent, as if a warm pearlescent light were glowing inside him, soft and subdued.

After that, I went to get a bottle of lavender body oil and a sewing kit from my bedroom. I applied the oil to the boy's body, on his chest, his arms, his stomach, his thin legs, between his toes. How fragile his body was, vulnerable in its naked compliance, as I tried to nudge it loose with heat, with my strength, the muscles under his skin rigid with the weight of death. Every part of his body a locus of remembrance: the whisker of a scar on his right kneecap from falling off his bicycle, the mole next to his navel, an 'ant' I tried to kill with my thumb whenever I gave him a bath, which would always send him into wild convulsions of giggles, a recent patch of rashes on his lower back for which I had just bought an antiseptic cream, still in its packaging in my hobo bag. How was it possible for a body to render so much, and yet to swiftly, unexpectedly, come to such an end, everything shutting down, coming to naught? Is the body nothing but a vessel, subject to time and its cruelties, its violence?

Later, taking up a needle and a dark thread, I started sewing up the gaping wounds on the boy's face, hands and chest. I went slowly, making sure that every cut, every tear, was stitched properly, the seams even and straight. It took a while, a whole night in fact, but I was not in any rush to complete this final task.

Yes, I sewed him up.

I just couldn't stand to see the open wounds on him. I couldn't bear to see him go in such a state.

When did I learn how to sew?

Yes, my mother did forbid me to sew, to pick up the needle.

But I learnt it anyway, secretly, without her knowledge.

Why? 'Cause it was something she had forbidden.

Didn't I always obey her?

Yes.

What can I tell you?

Because it was forbidden, disallowed, that's why.

She didn't know, I don't think so. She never found out.

It's not important now.

The thin thread I used to sew up the boy's wounds broke easily with a few tugs—it was suitable for cloth but not human skin, which is tougher, more resistant—and I had to pick through my wardrobe for a material that was thicker, stronger. In the end, I chose an old black woollen cardigan. I cut the edge of a corner and unravelled the weave until three-quarters of the cardigan was reduced to a bundle of threads. Slowly, I sewed up each of the wounds, checking and ensuring that the skin did not pucker up where the edges met, keeping the stitches neat

and tight. For the larger wounds, I had to trim away the loose
flaps of flesh with a small embroidery scissors so that the needle
could an old black on tauter skin. When I was finished, I ran
my fingers across the trails of dark stitches on the boy's body,
smoothing out its roughness. The boy was whole again, flawed
but intact, restored under my hand.

Then I applied another round of body oil on these stitches as
a final touch.

Finally, the boy was ready.

And he was so beautiful.

So quiet and still. At peace. Peaceful.

I think there is a kind of beauty you can only achieve in death,
something that can only be granted through death.

I could look at him the whole day.

It'd be my due.

What happens to a body when it dies? It's taken from you,
put away, hidden from sight. It no longer has any meaning or
significance or value, beyond the fact of its expiration. It's a
presence that has transmuted into an absence, a weight as indelible
and invisible as a shadow cast. The body was no longer the boy's,
but the boy was evident in every part of the body, and each part
spoke of his previous existence, his very being. Did I dream him
up, or was his existence truly material, a fact and a reality? Did
he truly move and breathe and laugh during all the years he had
lived—or had I imagined it?

For a long time after that, I could hardly remember the boy,
every thought of him silent and dormant, as if every image or
memory I had of him were dammed behind an impenetrable
wall, and I was denied any kind of access. Why couldn't I recall
a single thing about him? Was he really gone? I took out all the
photo albums and studied every photo I had taken of him over
the years—baby, toddler, child—and even then I still failed to

register him fully in my mind, as if the very person in the photos were merely a stand-in, someone in disguise, enacting different roles. I could not connect what I was seeing in these old photos to what was missing in my head, a stark blankness against a void, nothing upon nothing.

And then, one day, I felt him in the house, his presence. I began to smell traces of him in the air, and everything came back.

Yes, I know that now. He never really left.

Is he here now?

Where?

I can't see him, I can't see anything.

Where do I look?

I'll stop moving my head around if you stop touching it. I don't need your help.

Okay, I'll keep still.

The pain, horrible, like a ball of spikes, will it ever go away?

Yes, you're right, he's still here.

I can smell him now, that sweet milky scent of him.

Am I imagining it?

No, you're lying.

I always knew the girl had a deceptive, manipulative streak. She would lie to me all the time, but I knew enough to play along with her lies. She would complain about a pain in her stomach and refuse to eat, and I would rub Axe oil on her stomach and give her half of a Panadol. Still she would put up the pretence, doubling over in pain, a rather convincing performance with her pale icy face and trembling lips. How I would respond in kind, playing my part in the farce, a concerned mother, anxiety permeating my features, as I carried out my duties—fetching a glass of water, laying my hand on her tummy, rubbing, cooing endearments. Her dim eyes would track mine, troubled and apprehensive, as if considering her next move, the missing lines in her script, lost without a direction. *Are you feeling better*, I'd coo, sealing the doubt in her fretting, silencing it with a firm, decisive hand.

Another time, it would be her eyes—she could not stop rubbing them, they're so itchy—or an ulcer in her mouth, under her tongue. There was always something wrong with her, some small illness plaguing her body. When my patience was low or I wasn't in a mood to entertain her faked conditions, I'd leave her alone, locking her up in the room. The girl would cry and put up a fierce tantrum, knocking down the table and chair in the bedroom, tearing up the bedsheet and blanket—she had used the edge of a hair clip, poking a hole in the fabric, ripping it down the length—and pounding on the door, screaming like a wild beast, profanities and all. Where and how she acquired such a rich vocabulary—perhaps from the man, her father, with that tongue of his, I thought, bemused. Since then I had confiscated and removed any object that might pose such a danger, making my rounds of her room every day, checking and thoroughly assessing the potential threat and harm each item might cause, counting and recounting all the pencils I had given her to use for the day. No staplers or paper clips or ruler were allowed. I even went to the extent of trimming her nails every few days lest they grew too long or sharp. In any case, I would wait out her tantrum, till she had expended all her energy and then enter the room and tell her in as calm a voice as I could muster: *If you don't behave, don't expect anything from me, so quit your nonsense or else.* Her sapped face, when she looked up at me from the floor, down on her knees in exhaustion or frustration, was an ugly, hideous mask of contrition and fear, her eyes begging mine for leniency. *Now, clear up your own shit.*

Yet, despite my own behaviours towards the girl, harsh and necessary, punitive at times, I could, in a different light, see that the girl was a mirror of my own self in some way, as a child. On many occasions, she knew how to quickly read the temperature of the room, the surroundings—mostly my moods, which set and determined my interactions with her—and would react suitably, a shrewd, astute learner. After the early phase of throwing tantrums when she first arrived at the house, the girl managed to quieten down after a brief adjustment period, slowly becoming more watchful, observant. She started to ask questions, simple and unobtrusive, as if she were trying to find her bearing, to figure out her part in the overall scheme of things. She smiled more and even giggled at some of the things I said, her bright eyes crinkling with childish glee. How delighted she had seemed, how guileless—and how clever. She began to spend more time at the study table, drawing and writing and colouring, picture after picture, of people standing in front of a house with a huge orange sun and white billowing clouds hanging in the blue sky. The boy had the same creativity phase, drew the same stock pictures, stalks of sunflowers as tall as the house, along with rainbows and birds and giant worms, against a green field or a brown barren emptiness, a rote exercise picked up from kindergarten, all of which I had kept in large clear folders and put away in a drawer in my walk-in wardrobe. Unlike the boy, the girl was adept at colouring within the lines, the colours clearly segregated, rarely crossing boundaries, hiding any unsightly smudges with a thicker coat of chalk or shading. There was always a dog in her pictures. *Why*, I once asked her, pointing it out. *Because I have one, he's called Benny*, the girl said, *he really likes to lick my face, my hands, so cute.*

Sometimes, in an indulgent mood, I would buy her new toys—I did not think she would have liked the toys that belonged to the boy, cars and planes and trucks and trains of all sizes and varieties, which I had packed into storage boxes and put aside in the storeroom—a Barbie with hazel-brown skin and long black hair or an L.O.L Surprise doll, all glitter and saucer-eyed, and she would thank me for them, putting her hand on mine, a small deliberate gesture. Was she always like that or did she pick this up along the way, during her time in the house, to get me to lower my guard? I don't know.

Later, after she had more or less settled down and got used to the routine I had set for her, paying heed to all the expectations I'd laid down. That's when the girl wanted to play those silly hide-and-seek games, which I was happy to oblige. I knew what she was doing, the silly, obvious plan she was devising, but I played dumb. Just as long as I made sure the front door and metal gates were locked and the keys were with me, in my pocket. She could run and hide anywhere she wanted in the house, for as long as she wanted; in the end, I could always find her or get her to surrender. There was no way she could ever leave the house under my tight supervision. I would not let it happen again.

But still the girl was a bag of tricks, an opportunistic chameleon, and I was often taken aback by the sudden change in her demeanour, sometimes overnight. The most surprising transformation I had witnessed happened shortly after I caught her talking to herself in her room, at the tea party with her dolls. She had made up her bed that morning and changed out of her pyjamas without my prompting—the pyjamas were even folded, clumsily, a child's touch, and placed at the foot of her bed—her room tidy for once, the soft toys lined up against the pillows like a row of frigid sentries. She was already sitting at the edge of the bed when I looked in early to check on her, thinking she would still be asleep at six-thirty. But no, she was awake, her teeth brushed, her hair straightened out, hands on her lap, fingers interlaced. *What are you doing up so early?* I had asked. *Nothing, waiting for you*, she replied, *is breakfast ready? I'm hungry.*

Throughout the day, she did everything she was told, following my instructions and bidding to a tee—not unusual on most days, since, as I had previously mentioned, she was very astute and sharp-witted, and I, on my part, would not hesitate to correct her and mete out punishment, if necessary, to get her to obey—keeping out of the way when I left her alone, staying in her room, quiet like a mouse. She didn't play any games that day, no hide-and-seek, no tea parties. Her boxes of crayons and coloured pencils remained untouched, the sheaf of paper blank. I doubted she even got up from where she was seated, on the side of the bed, whenever I checked on her. Still, she would answer when I called out to her, come out of her room when I summoned her.

At first I took this as a clear unmistakable sign that she had finally come to terms with what was going on, resigning herself to the circumstances, but I grew uncertain after taking a long good look at her, sensing deep in my gut that something was off, like a small, vital object in a room suddenly removed, misplaced. In her eyes, I could still detect a knowing glint, and beyond that, a hint of something darker, a new awareness. She had smiled sweetly at me when I put my hand on her forehead, her face, checking for a temperature—again, her hand on mine, that smile, the vacant, unblinking gaze—and diverted my questions of concern. She had shrugged her shoulders, and assured me that she was fine.

I left her to her scheme, her new game. Something was up, I knew, the girl was hatching some new trick in her head. She was too easy to read, to predict. From time to time, I would linger quietly outside her room, trying to pick out what she was doing in there, whether she was mumbling to herself again. When she was, her voice was lower than usual, her words muffled, as though she were having some sort of conversation, a dialogue. In a soft voice, I'd hear her issuing questions and, pressing my ear closer to the door, I would try to make out something from the gap of silence that ensued. Nothing, and then the girl's voice would pipe up again, her tone slightly raised, yet another question. Why was she doing this, what was she possibly thinking of achieving with such a ruse? In any case, the girl kept up the pretence of her new game for days after, never once letting up and, oddly enough, also not letting me into the game, as if I were not a part of the original design, a key consideration in her deception.

Yes, I heard you, from inside the room.

What did I hear?

Everything. I missed nothing.

What were you pretending to do? Was it just some game you're playing?

Yes, you and your stupid childish games.

So, I lost the game?

But I'm not even playing it.

Did I start all this?

I don't think so.

You're very good at what you're doing. You almost had me convinced, fooled.

Where did you learn to do such a thing?

Imaginary conversations. That's a good one, old but effective.

Oh, look at me, I'm talking to an imaginary friend.

Am I crazy?

Not half as crazy as you would like me to be.

The girl is very much like the man, in ways that became more apparent as I got to know her over the weeks and months. Besides the evident physical resemblance—a short, stout build, a rosy oval face, large, sultry eyes—the girl also possesses the man's quick turn of mind, a way of assessing every situation with one's advantages or benefits in mind, a predatory nature. Like the man, she knows what she can get away with if she tries, for the other alternative—to not get what she wants even if she tries—is unbearable to her, an opportunist's loss. Her cunning is quite something to behold, for someone her age, and I can only imagine what she can be, what she can do, as she matures, as her mind sharpens. In a world full of crafty, manipulative men with their tyranny and oppression, her wiles would take her far, so far, and yield for her what have been missing from my own life: autonomy, agency, self-belief.

Ah, but she's just a child, still a child, I had to remind myself. What does a child know? What's the world to a child, a girl, a pampered one at that, but something soft and cushy, easy to handle, to understand, a place safe and protected, with nothing too hard or complicated to wrap her mind around? The world's her oyster, and she, the hard white pearl at the heart.

I had to keep an eye on the girl for some time before I finally made my move. Observing her at the park with the maid, or at the quadrangle in school with her classmates playing tag, or at her Chinese enrichment class at the shopping mall, making notes of everything she did, what she wore, her interactions with others. Even from a distance, her personality was clearly perceptible, like a spark rising from the embers. How she could command the people around her with her charm and ease—a bright smile, an innocuous laugh, her artful deference. While studying her at play with her classmates—how the other girls would monkey noisily around her, like eager subjects, seeking her attention, paying tributes—I could not help but feel a thrill at recognizing something I saw in the man; how he, too, could easily get the team at the agency excited about a new project, or to come around to his ideas, his suggestions, with hardly any effort at all. How he would rally the troops, much like how the girl was doing, to follow his lead, to bow to his authority. The apple doesn't fall far from the tree, it seemed, a realization that came to me during the long hours I spent tracking the girl from school to home, from activity to activity, with the maid or with the family, never alone. And it dawned on me that to get to the man, to really make him see or feel anything, I had to first get the girl.

Yes, to get to the man.

Why? 'Cause he didn't know what he had, he never did. He took things, people, for granted. Our relationship, what we have, our lives together. He didn't care at all.

So what if he did get me this house, which he had thought I wanted.

But it's only because I thought we could make a life here, together.

Yes, he already has a family, I know that.

But he promised a new one with me.

Yes, of course, I believed him then.

How would I know he'd never leave his family for me?

He'd wanted to, he told me, so many times, in the early days of our courtship.

He had so much to lose? What about me then? Don't I stand to lose just as much? Maybe even more.

Yes, he doesn't know a thing about losing. He doesn't know what it feels like to lose something, someone, to have it ripped out of your own heart.

Is that why I brought you here?

Yes.

To make him suffer.

To make him see.

Why didn't I tell him about the boy then? Because his death would have meant nothing to him.

No, he didn't deserve to know. He never really cared about the boy after he was born.

I only told him because I had no other choice.

That I was pregnant.

To have a child at my age was the furthest thing in my mind at the time. I had only just started on my first job, fresh out of school, which was turning out better than I had expected, with the promotion and small pay raise after a year. It was my first taste at what I had hoped would be a long career in advertising: copywriter, then art director, creative director, who knows what was possible, what could lie ahead. I had the smarts—I graduated second in my cohort, made the dean's list—and the drive and determination, I was clear about my goals and I wanted more—experience, exposure, and everything that came with it: success, recognition, money, a good life. If there was one thing I learnt from my mother, it was the ethics of being completely self-sufficient, to not depend on anyone for anything. *If you depend on people, they would always disappoint you, no matter what*, my mother never ceased to remind me. *Learn to survive on your own, not on others.* With that credo in mind, my mother had remained a seamstress, self-employed, till the day she died, working on her own terms, with no one she had to answer to, free to make all her decisions, her choices. Life was hard, money scarce, options very limited—*but what did you expect*, she would say, *life handed to you in a little basket, all nice and tidy, is it, and what use would you have of it?* To be independent, self-sufficient, to earn one's keep were something of tremendous pride to my mother, a thing she had held close to her heart—her ability to give me a proper education, to keep us clothed and sheltered and fed, to never, ever, depend on any man for anything. It was a thing branded on me since young, something I had learnt by heart, by the force and example and the brutal will of my mother. And for a long time, after she committed suicide, it was the only thing that had kept me going: *survive, you have to survive, you will survive.*

Still, the chips fall where they may, and things took a sudden turn, despite my late mother's admonishment and my best efforts. Where I had failed: I fell in love with the man. It wasn't something I had foreseen or wanted for myself, so early in my life, but then it happened: a long gaze and a wandering, and the mind fell headlong into a dark hole. My first love, an office affair, an illicit relationship, like a series of connected dominoes, one falling after the other, ineluctable. What would my mother have thought of this, if she were alive to witness it, how she would have laughed and then beat the idea out of me before I made the mistake— *Don't be foolish! Don't ever think a man can give you everything, you hear? That would be your downfall, to think a man can love you, look at yourself!* She would have locked me up, whipped me to shreds, cut my hair, sliced my face, crippled me, just to stop me from seeing the man again. She would have shown me the terrible blunder I'd have made, her acts justifying her love and all the punishments she would mete out would be nothing compared to the consequences I had yet to see and would be unable to bear.

The truth of my mother's beliefs had been borne out by her own experiences. Though she had never brought up the subject of my father when I was growing up, it was clear from her actions that whatever she did was to repudiate any lingering effects of her own failed marriage caused by my father's callous act of desertion. *Men can't be trusted, men are useless, men only want to use you up and toss you aside*, my mother would say, her voice breathless with rage, caught up in one of her explosive episodes. Behind the shadow of any man lay the ghost of my father, haunting the halls and rooms of my mother's mind.

Once, I had shown her a photo taken during a class outing to the Science Centre when I was in primary six, pointing to a classmate standing two rows behind me. I told her how the boy was always teasing me in school and playing pranks on me, pulling my hair or dropping eraser shavings down the back of my shirt. My mother had snatched the photo out of my hand and torn it to pieces. *Don't even think about boys now, you'll ruin yourself*, she had said before slapping me out of my daze, and later eliciting a solemn assurance out of me to never talk to that boy again.

Every desire I had ever felt was crushed by my mother with a harsh word or beating. Even when it was something as innocent as a young girl's puppy love for a Japanese or Korean pop star, gleaned from the tittle-tattle of my classmates and the glossy magazines that were passed around during lesson breaks. I'd lap up everything written in these magazines, the scandals and messy love affairs of the celebrities, their lavish clothes, their extravagant lifestyles, memorizing their faces, their looks, the happiness etched on their bright, shiny exteriors, since my mother had forbidden me to spend any money on such trash that would rot the brain. The occasional Chinese newspapers with their lurid headlines that my mother bought on weekends were meant solely for her to check the latest 4D results or lottery, a small vice she sometimes allowed herself, to try her luck. While my classmates would gush and swoon over these singers and actors tirelessly, exchanging gossips and graffiting the pages of their textbooks and exercise books with silly pledges of love and adoration for them, I'd smile and remain quiet, keeping my head down, my thoughts to myself. From them, I'd learn who was hot, who was dud, who was filthy rich, who was irresistible, who would make a perfect boyfriend, the one to love forever. I never joined in their banter, unsure how to talk about someone whom I had not met or known, despite what was endlessly written about them, having no sense of what my feelings for them should be, besides a general sense of awe and disbelief at their wealth, the flashiness of their unbelievable lives, like a rare species of mammals I had read about in a science reference book, famed for their size or trait or unique ability. When teased, I'd spit out the name of the most popular member of the latest Korean boy band, liked by majority of my female classmates, just to throw them off the scent. There was hardly any need to make known my true feelings, which, when it's all boiled down, came to nothing but an empty well, long dried of water.

Through my secondary and later junior college years, I had wanted nothing to do with boys, or men, for fear that what my mother had said was true, that they were sly, conniving creatures, setting up their baits and traps, waiting to cause me harm and lead me to my downfall. I had to stay alert and watchful around my male classmates, not to show any emotion or wayward feelings towards them, or let them get too close to me. It was unavoidable to rub shoulders with them during school projects and group assignments, but I had managed to keep a proper, appropriate distance, bridging the gap with my shy demeanour, my silent ways. After I rejected them many times, to go for a meal at McDonald's or hang around at a mall, they soon lost their patience and goodwill and left me alone like I wished. I was the quiet one, the one who would never raise her hand in class, the one to take down every note the teachers wrote on the whiteboard, always staying on the sidelines, watching and listening but never intrusive, never prying, eager to rush back home after school ended. My adolescence was a long drought of loneliness that never found any relief. By the time I came out of it, I was already moulded into someone used to being alone, to seek her own solitude, her solace.

Yet, the relentless eyes of the boys never really left me, keeping me within their close surveillance, marking me out for their spoils, their taking: sweet and pleasant, cold and detached, mediocre and unresponsive, slut or virgin. I was held up to their scrutiny, their dissection, every time I walked past them, the faces turning to me with a cool, insouciant stare, levelling a frank, undisguised appraisal. Even when I chose to be alone, I was never truly out of someone's—a boy's—gaze, incessantly assessed and judged on many levels, measured against invisible, unspoken standards. A girl is a thing with many parts, readily given to be taken apart, to be devoured. Once in secondary school, and twice in college, I had been approached by boys with an intention to woo me, but these I had turned down decisively, either with a bland refusal or a polite rejection. None of them took these rejections personally or seriously, brushing it off with a what-the shrug or a self-effacing grin, quick to bounce back, for I would see them, in a few weeks' time, with another classmate, 'going steady', leaning into each other's bodies during recess, a new glow on their faces. Outside of school, I'd see them holding hands, mushy with words, struck dumb with the aura of newborn love. It had not mattered who the object of love was, which could skip from person to person, ranging like a vane in the wind, pointing in any direction; the substance of a pursuer's love can only take the shape, fill the form of a willing, expectant recipient. Love, if it were love I was witnessing back then, is nothing more than a game of musical chairs, people spinning round and round, hunting for empty seats. Truth be told, it would have been unthinkable to get close to anyone, with my mother constantly on my back, her words ringing in my ears.

The man was the first man I became intimate with, four months after my mother's suicide. I had not planned to find anyone, let alone fall in love with someone; a few girlfriends had tried in vain to fix something up for me—movies and dinners with their friends, brothers or cousins, double dates with their boyfriends' friends, to which I had expressed little or no interest. I was just coming into my own, freshly graduated, with a new exciting job to boot. And then, the unexpected blow of my mother's death, which threw everything into disarray, flipping my whole life inside out. I was finally cut off, unmoored, set adrift. A large, indeterminable part of me was broken—no, severed—by my mother's sudden absence, and the affair I had with the man, who barrelled right into my life like a gale of irresistible force, felt like the start of something real and monumental, a vital, necessary step into a completely different life from the one I had for so long. I was deeply lonely and in pain and half out of my mind with grief then that I would have given anything to feel just a bit of something—kindness, affection, maybe even pity, from anyone. The man offered a fort in which I could take refuge and hide all my terrible feelings.

It was less than ten months after our affair began that I realized I was pregnant. Things had been going well between the man and I—we had talked about going on longer overseas trips then, to Kyoto and Barcelona, and the man had even proposed getting a new place for me to stay; I was, at the time, still living in the old one-room flat whose ownership had been transferred to my name after my mother's death, and had complained to him on several occasions about how I wanted to move out if I had the chance or means—and I had begun to imagine the life and future we could have together. Having kids played a very small, insignificant part in the fantasy I had, a peripheral decorative feature of my imaginings, though, god forbid, I wanted any at the time.

And then, what do you know, I was pregnant, and everything became all too real, all of a sudden. What was I to do with a child, at my age? I was only twenty-two and had yet to make anything out of my life. Fears rose like thorns, pricking my mind. In my heart, I did not want to be like my mother, who had lived a sad, hardscrabble life, saving and scrimping to keep us alive, with, in the end, nothing to her name. She had known no other way out of her misery, except to burrow herself in the only work she knew, to sew, and to take out all her unhappiness and frustration on me, her only child. She had left nothing behind, nothing of value. I had thrown out nearly all of her possessions when I moved from the flat into the new house, retaining only a few of her personal items for keepsakes that barely filled a small wooden box, which I had kept somewhere in the walk-in closet, sealed and untouched. Whatever she had left for me, in me, the long years and the memories, I had not wanted any of it, pushing them out of my mind, reducing her existence to something I could manage, a vivid character in a story that I had read a long time ago, nothing more. You exist only as long as the last person who remembers you, I once read, about the last living person of a long-lost tribe, bringing all that he knew about his culture, people, and language, into the grave when he dies, everything gone—what would such a loss be, I wondered, for an entire race to cease to exist, and to be the only one left to witness its demise, its death? I had wanted not to remember my mother—no, not like what she was in the later years, her cruelty and her pain—and yet I couldn't get her out of my mind, not quite. To be the last one alive, to remember, is to bear with all that came before, the weight of the past, the burden of history.

And yet, all that I took away from my mother's life and meaningless death was the lesson to never be like her. *I didn't work so hard for you to be like me.* Through her sacrifices, I had gained an education, a mind of my own, choices, which would have ensured that our paths would never be the same—a different, better life within reach, a guarantee. So, to become a mother was to kill all my best-laid plans, to rob my life of its potential and possibilities. I could not have imagined a worse fate.

But the man had wanted to keep it after I told him the news. *But what about me*, I told him, *what about my job, what's going to happen to it.* The man shrugged his shoulders and said: *We would cross the bridge when we come to it.* To abort the baby was out of the question for both of us; it was not something I was capable of, the idea of killing my own child, my flesh and blood—the thought itself was unthinkably savage—and for the man, his conscience, which could not bear the strain of the consequences. *A child is a child, and it's mine, and I'll take care of you and the baby*, the man had assured me as the days ticked past the first trimester.

I had to keep my pregnancy a secret at work, wearing looser clothes as the months progressed—thankfully the bump did not show much, not until the sixth month, which triggered another frantic round of shopping, not for maternity clothes, no, which would have been a dead giveaway, but for baggy dresses and sweaters with shapeless fit, and a good number of shawls and wraps for additional cover—and, when it became too obvious, at least to my naked eye, I took an extended leave of absence—citing the need to attend to an urgent family matter—for several months, which was duly supported and approved by the man. No one in the office suspected anything; only once did a female colleague casually tease me about my fleshy cheeks, which I was quick to laugh off, blaming my weight gain on the excess of snacks in the pantry that I couldn't help bingeing. In the months leading up to the birth of the boy, when I holed myself up in the house like a recluse, the man was constantly dropping by on visits, after work and sometimes during lunch hours, bringing all the things I asked for: groceries, DVDs, magazines, toiletries, takeaways of certain food that I was craving, endless assurance. He knew exactly how to play his part in all of this, and to his credit, he was flawless in his role and performance.

So, he's a good father? To you?

Yes, I can tell. I'd seen the way he played with you, how he always indulged you, caved in to whatever you wanted.

The apple of his eye. The only one that mattered.

Does he love the boy? Maybe. It's a son, after all.

Am I too old to think this way? Sons are better than daughters?

You know what they say about daughters being ex-lovers of fathers?

Don't laugh, it's true. Don't you believe it?

I know you do. He's so in love with you. One look, and anyone can tell.

What kind of father is he to the boy?

An adequate one, good enough, I think.

It doesn't take much to be a good father for only an hour or two a day. You just play with your kid and be the good guy, the fun parent.

Oh, he wasn't around much? Always at work?

Ah, the lies he told.

Maybe he was with me, maybe he was with someone else. I don't know. I can never get him to stay for long, not even after I gave birth to the boy.

Yes, he did promise to take care of me and the boy.

But only with the things he could buy, with what he could afford.

He likes to compensate like that, with things, possessions, to make up for his absence.

Yes, he does.

The boy grew up in the wavering shadows of the man's presence, which came and went like bouts of seasonal rain, here for a while then gone. In his absence, and to his credit, the man did what he could to alleviate my burdens as a young first-time mother by hiring a full-time nanny and a part-time housekeeper who came by thrice a week to take care of the household chores of washing and cleaning and cooking. The nanny, a Malaysian woman in her early fifties, was kind and accommodating, very hands-on with all the tasks revolving around the baby, instructing and guiding me through the essential things I needed to do: what to feed the baby to get him to poo more, how to massage the Eucalyptus oil on the baby's tummy in a certain way to relieve his discomfort, how to hold his head at an angle so his mouth would latch on tighter to my nipple. Her maternal solicitousness came on display as she plied me with tonics and brews and soups that reeked of ginger and dark sauces, and waved me off to rest, to sleep whenever the baby started to bawl. For a great part in the early months of my new motherhood, I barely had to handle the baby, besides the regular periods of breastfeeding and watching him sleep after each feeding, leaving most of the care-taking to the nanny. I'd sneak up to his cot from time to time to watch him, but mostly he would be sound asleep, his arms tucked into the band of the oversized bottoms, his mouth half open in a tiny O. And when he cried or became too fussy, the nanny would be on hand to minister to him, to change his nappy, to coo to him, to put him in a better posture to sleep. I was often told to rest more, to recuperate, to get my strength back. *Both of you, so young,* the nanny once said, half in jest, teasing, *like babies, who will take care of who.* I had rolled my eyes then and smiled, trying but failing to ignore her comment, the sting of it sinking into me. Still, at the back of my mind, I feared and dreaded the day she would be gone, and I would be left completely alone with the baby—what would I do then, how would I manage? A few times, in the throes of utter fatigue after a long day, I'd sweep my gaze to the nanny holding the crying baby in her thick arms, her mouth close to his ears, and have sharp, fleeting visions of my mother cradling the baby, rocking him back to sleep, her eyes glinting with a joy I had never seen before. My mother, now a grandmother. How the sudden thoughts of her would pierce my heart, straight through, blade and hilt. How I would weep silently into the pillow, till the nanny, sensing my distress, would come to me, her hand on my head, my arm, stroking, saying, *it's okay, don't worry, every new mum goes through this stage, it's hard now but you'll get used to it, you'll be fine, the baby will be fine, you'll be a good mother.*

The housekeeper, on the other hand, was younger, not by much, perhaps in her mid-forties, and possessed a canny, cunning personality, and a nosey nature that she softly disguised with an astute and calculated approach to the things she did and said. While thorough in handling and discharging her chores around the house, completing them well within the allocated hours of the day, she could sometimes come across as being overly zealous, overextending her influence in the house, bringing us, this small group of women, under her direction. The way we would leave the clothes all over the floor for her to pick up, the dirty dishes we left overnight on the dining table instead of soaking them in the sink, all the endless things she had to pick up after us—she never came at me with these complaints; instead, they would come as crisp scoldings and retorts, all directed at the nanny who would blindly relay them back to me. All I got from the housekeeper, as a way of passive-aggressive retaliation, was a decisive bang of the bathroom cabinet, the gush of water running at full tap, the brisk loud washing, the tsk-tsk-ing of tongue under her breath, the quick averting of her eyes before I could finish a word with her. I knew what she must have thought as she went around cleaning the huge house: how did I, a young ignorant woman, barely out of school, get to live in such a big fancy house with a new baby? What had I done to deserve this? What was my relationship to the man? On the last point, it was hard to ignore her blatant curiosity—observing from the corner of my eyes, pretending to be asleep or distracted—as she tided the master bedroom, putting away stray pieces of laundry, peeking into the drawers, scanning the contents. Sometimes, coming into one of the rooms or the kitchen, I would chance upon the housekeeper and nanny, heads leaning into each other, talking in hushed tone, and swiftly breaking up upon seeing me, scattering into other rooms, turning back to their duties, one with a suppressed knowing grin, the other with a sheepish, guilty look. In time, I would reduce the days that I needed the housekeeper around, gradually cutting down the hours till she only had to come by once a week for three hours, during which

I'd task her with a long list of menial chores to do, to complete, while keeping my eye on her the entire time.

On the days he visited, the man would bring me huge bags and parcels of clothes and accessories and baby products, and spend some time carrying and feeding and playing with the baby. It was evident from his face that he took a great delight in the boy—a son, no less, his son—and would spare no effort to give him what he needed. He insisted on buying the best baby formula, just as I was starting to wean the boy off milk, a can costing nearly close to a hundred dollar, a carton of it each time. Onesies, footies, bodysuits, pyjamas, rompers—'Cutest Boy Ever!' 'I ♥ Mum'—all crammed into drawers and shelves of the cupboards in the baby's room, half of which still in their packaging and carrier bags, price tags affixed, already too small for the boy by the time I got to them. No matter how much I threw out, the man continued to buy more, splurging as if his life depended on it, his paternal care manifested in requisite providence. I, too, got a share of what his money could buy—a Cartier Trinity bracelet, a Tiffany solitaire diamond pendant, a pair of Souveraine de Chaumet earrings in white gold. *Nothing but the best for you, the new mother*, the man said, presenting these gifts like tributes, hiding them under the pillow or in the drawer of my vanity table. I would gush and get myself worked up over these gifts, not because I wanted them—why did he think I'd want such things anyway? Where would I ever have a chance to wear them in my current state, burdened with the baby, trapped at home all the time? What was he thinking, really?— but because it was the natural response to give, an appreciative, performative gesture, a role to keep up. At the back of my mind I wondered if he had done the same for his wife too. Had he also made such grand efforts to please her, for giving him a daughter? Nonetheless, I still went to the trouble of wearing these pieces whenever he came over, trying to doll myself up—pale and fat and ugly, saggy everywhere—as best as I could, feeling like a sow in pearls.

On his birth certificate, I had given the boy my surname, after the man had refused my request to put down his name as the boy's father. *I know he's my son, and that's good enough,* he had said, brushing aside my insistence. We had quarrelled furiously over the matter—I, standing my ground initially, weakening as time went by, and he, sounding the right words, punctuating his stubborn decision with a slam of the door, an opportune exit—before I finally consented and did what I was told. I did not want to strain our relationship any further; the birth of the boy had already taken a toll on us, as I'd expected, and so the boy remained fatherless in the eye of the law. Had I already failed him then, failed to give him what was rightfully his, a surname, his one connection to his father?

On the days that the man was gone, I would hug the boy and look at him, my mind racked with doubt and fear, and wish that things could have been different for him, only if I were a stronger woman, a worthier mother. He deserved someone better, someone who would put him at the centre of her life, the sun around which her very being, her survival, depended. Yet, even then, gazing into his sweet lovely face, I could not help but feel the sharp, opposing desire of wanting something more, something else, than this life, a life weighed down by the ever-urgent needs of another: the feeding, the wiping, the tending to. In the darkest of moods—was I like my mother in such moments, I sometimes wondered, her spirit spurred awake inside me, coming alive—I would curse every choice that I had ever made that had brought me to this very point, to this plight. Had my mother felt the same way too when she had me at such a young age? Did she also feel that her own life had been taken—robbed, snatched, stolen, any form of theft, really—from her? Was that why she was so angry all the time?

Looking at the boy, with these warring feelings clashing inside me, I often felt my own rage rising swiftly to the surface, taking over my rationale, subsuming it, and the thought of doing the unfathomable, the inexplicable, would briefly flash across my mind—it would be a simple deed, to pinch the boy's nose or to let him fall from my hands, to snuff out a life. I could do it just like that, with a snap of a finger, without any thought or preamble. But the moment my mind crossed over to the other side, I was immediately seized by a grip of terrible remorse—how could I possibly think such a thought, what kind of a monster was I?

Now, is that the truth you wanted to hear?

Yes, go ahead, laugh all you want.

Yes, a monster.

It's so convenient to put a name, a tag, to something that scares you, isn't it? To someone you do not know, or don't care to know. Makes it easy to know what's what.

What's wrong with being a monster?

If you were me, you would have done the same thing too.

Then what would you call yourself?

Now, you're making me laugh.

Wait, let me catch my breath.

Better.

I went back to work three months after the birth of the boy, and had a very hard time adjusting to the rush and rhythm of the office. New clients, new colleagues, tighter timelines, smaller budgets. I kept finding myself distracted at every little thing, constantly frustrated by my expanded job scope, taking on the work of a colleague who had gone on maternity leave, the never-ending meetings and debriefs. I had thought that a break from the months of pregnancy and rest was what I had needed—I was feeling choked by the pressing demands of being a new mother—and yet, in the office, surrounded by the grating squawk of my colleagues and the noisy bustle of routines and deadlines, I started hankering for the other life I had left behind—not with the baby, no, but the soft, buoyant period shortly after my mother's death when I was alone and wrecked, but alive and sensitive to every possibility that lay ahead of me. I was free to do whatever I wanted, to go anywhere I felt like, and meet anyone I liked—I was free, untethered, after so many years of being under the straitlaced, ironclad rule of my mother. With my salary, I could have saved enough to travel, go places, live a little; I did not have to live for anyone or anything. There was nothing holding me back—until now. As I meandered through the long hours in the office, transiting from one meeting to another, taking breaks from round after round of copywriting and vetting and rewrites, these were the thoughts that held me in a fugue-like daze, pulling me back to a time that had already slipped from my hands. Like a fantasy that had long been killed, its ghost continued to haunt me, to trail in my wake.

Even then, I held on to my job for a while. I put in the necessary hours, staying late into the night to complete all my tasks at work—perhaps I was not trying hard enough, I told myself, perhaps I need more time to get back into the swing of things. I knew my work, I had the skills, I was competent. Since the boy was taken care of by the nanny then—the man had extended her contract, offering a big raise, even a small bonus to sweeten the deal—I was not worried about him. When I came home late at night and sneaked into the boy's bedroom—we had moved his cot into another room, just down the corridor from the master bedroom, a room painted in Persian blue with custom-made shelves and furnishings, a constellation of glow-in-the-dark stars streaking across the walls and ceiling, the nanny sleeping on a makeshift mattress next to the cot—he would already be asleep, wrapped snugly in a blanket, a cherubic angel. From the nanny, I would get an update of what had happened during the day, what the boy did, what he ate, how long he slept, and hearing her reports was like receiving news from a place where I had been exiled. The boy learning to flip himself onto his stomach, to crawl a short distance, to pick up a soft ball. How wonderful, and distressing, it was to receive such anecdotes, my insides churning with grits of jealousy and resentment. Before dismissing the nanny for the night, I would give her some money, a small gesture of gratitude—and in some way, I feel, to assuage my own guilt. She would smile timidly at me, before tucking the money into the pocket of her shorts.

Naturally, the issue of me going back to work was a matter of contention between the man and I. He had wanted me to quit my job to take care of the boy—*Didn't I pay for everything you need? What else do you want?*—but I had refused, not ready or willing to give up yet another part of my life to accommodate the new role of a mother. I pushed against his decision time and again, and the rising friction soon gave way to a period of molten tension that tested both our resolves. The man coolly withdrew his attention from me as he simmered in his anger, turning his gaze away, and suddenly I found myself floundering, losing the courage to keep up the fight. *I can't do this by myself, I don't think I can,* the fears mounting inside me screamed. And then another voice—my mother's—would rise forth: *Because you're weak, you have always been weak.*

Maybe she's right. Maybe she had always been right about me.

After all, she had known me my whole life, had seen through me.

So you agree with her.

But there's really nothing I could do about the situation then, to change it.

No, I can't leave the man.

No, it's not so easy.

'Cause I need him.

Do our needs make us weak?

No, I think they make us human.

No, I don't think I have always been weak.

What did my mother know about being weak? All she had ever done was to exert her control over me, to keep me pinned under her thumb. Everything I did or said was scrutinized and criticized by her, relentlessly, interminably. Nothing was or could ever have been done right in her eye. Everything had to be corrected, remedied, any sign I showed of having a life or a mind of my own was trampled on, weeded out. Any thought or feeling I had was squashed, reduced to nil. Nothing good could ever come out of me. If anything, she was the one who had made me weak, made me doubt myself and question my every act, every decision.

Once, when I was fourteen and had threatened to run away if she hit me again, my mother had taken a kitchen knife and held it to her wrist and told me that if I were to ever attempt such a thing, she would cut herself and bleed to death and her death would be on my conscience. *Go ahead, run, see what I'll do*, she had said, and, to get her point across emphatically, she had poked the tip of the knife into her wrist, making a tiny slit in the skin, summoning the blood. On her face, she registered not an ounce of pain, her eyes dead, and looking directly into them, I had felt the thrill of sickening panic. For days afterwards, my mother would brandish her cut—she had refused to apply any medicine or to bandage it—whenever I was around, making sure I saw it clearly if I happened to glance at her, handing me a rag to wipe down the dining table or giving me my weekly allowance. She knew how to inflict a kind of pain that went beyond just beatings and physical punishments—a different brutality that built and rode on a person's guilt and shame, which was more effective, more potent, for such feelings never went away, only burrowing themselves deeper into the core, inextricable. I was the perpetrator, the one who caused my mother pain, the wilful, unfilial child; it was only fair that I had to bear witness to what I had done. What was at stake, what was needed on my part, the very thing that my mother had wanted was my full and total submission. Nothing else would have pleased her more. I gave in once, and I gave in again and again.

Yet my mother was never satisfied, always fearing that I would take a turn and fall away from her. Her suspicions, metastasizing into paranoia, overtook her mind, and she began to devise new ideas to kill herself—threatening to drink the toilet bleach, to jump from the flat, to walk into traffic—in order to keep me in my place, if I did the slightest thing to go against her wishes. *Why do you want to do this to me, why don't you listen, why can't you be good?* she would cry and beg, gripping my hair in her fist, grinding my face to the ground. *Do you really want to see me die, is that it, you want me to die?* Sometimes, staring at my mother at the height of her wild theatrics, I would imagine her taking the final step—driving the knife deeper into her wrist, taking a long gulp from the bottle of Clorox, throwing herself in front of a speeding truck—and feel a deep and tremendous sense of relief. At such times, I would dare her with a silencing stare: *Do it, kill yourself, see whether I care.*

It was no use fighting my mother when she was in her maniacal state, unhinged and uncontrollable. Like a rat hiding in a hole, I learnt to build my will and my strength from inside the walls of my weaknesses that I displayed to my mother. I learnt to mask my true feelings, my disgust, my contempt and, in place of these, to offer up something that could be taken as my submission, my deference. It got easier as I got older, to manage the constant shifting and adjustment of these disguises. Was there ever a true self that I could draw from, to make sense of the world around me, I wondered; perhaps, it's much easier to assume many selves, for I had never felt myself to be made up or tied down to a single idea of who I was. Understanding this and learning to live with it was my only way out of the narrow, squalid life I had with my mother, to allay and temper the barbed, tumultuous relationship we had. And yet, in the end, despite my veiled resistance and numerous guises, I still became the person she had created me to be, one forged in her very likeness.

Yes, like mother like daughter. I don't need you to tell me that.

Was I happy when she died?

I don't know.

Maybe.

My mother was shrewd enough to change her tactics once in a while to get me to submit, to yield. The soft approach, the carrot, for one. She would dress my cuts and wounds after the beatings, and cook a meal of dishes I liked: sweet and spicy spare ribs, salted egg prawns, lor mee with ngoh hiang. She spared no expense or effort to prepare these dishes. She would watch me eat, taking pleasure in my appetite, heaping my bowl with scoops of meats and prawns. Suppressing my nausea, I would bite down every morsel of food with a bitter swallow of blood, moulding my face into a presentable, placable mask, willing myself not to retch. Later, I'd let her take me into her arms, to stroke my hair—I never knew how to resist her, to push her away, when it came to this; perhaps secretly I had craved for it too, and wanted to believe she had a different side to her, a tender, more caring side, someone who had my best interests at heart—and calm me down with a half-remembered song from my childhood. A ditty about a baby elephant losing her way, trying to locate her herd, or a baby sparrow befriending a worm that didn't want to be eaten. Sometimes, mumbling along to her singing, I'd fall asleep on my mother's lap, slipping into oblivion.

Much as I hated her then, when the wounds were still fresh and I could still taste the blood on my lips, I could do nothing but be stirred, almost against my will, by my mother's kind, loving gestures. She could change, she was not herself, she cared deeply, she would be better, I told myself time and again, overcoming every part of me that screamed otherwise. Perhaps when you're hungry and starving all the time, you wouldn't mind what was being tossed at you, these tiny scraps of charity or pity that you lapped up without a thought, greedily, ravenously. It might never come again—and this was the fear that surfaced constantly, the scarcity and unpredictability of the source, the wilful withholding, the desultory dispensation—and so you took all that was given, every single pathetic crumb. I took everything my mother gave: tenderness, gentle ministrations, soft words. And over time, it became harder and harder to separate what was kind or cruel, good or manipulative, in what my mother did; perhaps every act of love carried a tiny seed of darkness inside. Was she, too, a woman of many selves—and did I really know which was which, where it truly mattered?

At times, when the days were especially bad, after she had exhausted her rage on me, my mother would pull me to her, lay her head on my lap and give herself over to long bouts of crying. I would put my hand on her head and rake my fingers through the long kinky grey strands and feel her tremors permeating the skin of my thighs, coursing up my body. How terrible she must have felt, how wretched to be tormented like she was, by her demons, unseen but overwhelming. The distance between us, bridged by our skin and touches, never failed to remind me of the sufferings my mother had to endure, though invisible to me but all too real to her. What had I not understood about her pain, what had I unwittingly ignored? When her cries gradually subsided, I would touch the arches of her thin brows and wipe her tears away. *I don't have much in life, you're all that I have, and all I want is for you to be good, to be obedient, to have everything,* my mother would say, staring up at me, beseechingly. I would look away then, not knowing where to place my eyes, absently stroking her hair. I would make an effort to drain my mind to a blank, to try not to take in her words or believe them—the moment of intense empathy, briefly stirred, quickly lapsed into a hardening, studied apathy, triggered by my mother's usual refrain, like an old dog, just fed, already growing wary of her mistress's cruelty, her mistreatment—but already they would have sneaked their way inside me and taken hold. My heart would churn and twist at her words, at the warmth seeping from her skin to mine. Would I ever stop believing her? I don't know. Even now, when life got too hard or things just seemed insurmountable, I could still hear my mother's voice, soft and pleading, calling out to me.

Yes, I can hear her.

All the time.

I just have to listen.

What does she say to me?

All that she needs to tell me. Her advice, her warnings. All her 'I told you so's'.

Yes, of course, I listen to her.

I've been listening to her all this while, even now.

I heard her when she told me how she felt about the man when I gushed about him, how smart he was, how charismatic, to her. *No, he'll ruin you if you let him*, she had said, sensing the turn of my unvoiced feelings towards him, like swift currents under the surface. *Don't believe a word he said, he's just trying to use you. Once he's done with you, he would dump you like he did with the other women.* How did she know about these other women—had she seen through the man, clearly and unambiguously, and had known what he was like, with the little that I had revealed to her? What had she read in my mind, in the thoughts that had yet to settle, that were still murky to me? I heard her every word but refused to take heed of it. *Stop it, you don't know what I want*, I told her, *all you want is for me to be unhappy, to feel miserable my whole damn life.*

She never stopped, not once, to express her disapproval, her castigations, at everything I did, her critical voice a constant presence in my head. When I first knew about the pregnancy, she was on my back, hounding me, shrieking at me to abort it, to get rid of the *little bastard.* Her voice, insistent, vexed, furiously nudging me to make the decision. *He already has a wife and kid, why would he want a child with you? You stupid fool, why can't you think for once, do you really want your child to be a bastard, do you?*

Still, I turned a deaf ear to her words, to block them out, and to run in the opposite direction. I could not shut her up, even when she was gone, dead, her words still resounding in my head.

Yes, she's very alive to me.

No, I can't quite get rid of her.

I can't, even if I try.

She's always with me.

My mother's condition continued to worsen over time, becoming more and more erratic, volatile, with even wilder mood swings. She would call me several times a day, only to scream at me: *where are you, what are you doing, who are you with, who is he, what are you doing with him, why are you not back yet, are you sleeping around, why are you such a slut, why can't you ever learn?* And then, having expended her burst of invective, she would hang up the phone on me and, a few minutes later, call again and beg me to come home: *please come home, please don't be angry with me, I'm sorry, have you eaten, do you want me to cook for you, do you have enough money, don't stay out too long, it's already late, I don't want you to get hurt, there are so many dangers out there, come back soon, quickly come home, I don't want to be alone.* On and on, she would entreat and cajole, urging me to listen, to be good, to take heed, her pitiful, needy self a shadow of what she was a moment ago when she had lashed out at me, all fire and venom. I never knew how to respond to her when she acted out like that, and so I took the simplest solution: I kept my silence.

And in keeping my silence and not responding in the way she had wanted—with sufficient contrition and shame—my mother took it out on me with even harsher beatings, putting in all her strength, her arms shivering with exertion at the end of each thrashing, her face flushed with green veins streaking from her temples into the hairline. In her eyes, a singular throb of madness, burning, flaring. By then, her escalating outbursts of rage and empty threats had meant very little to me, becoming useless and ineffectual, and only further exposed her own neediness and vulnerability. My mother had needed me to play my part, to stick to the script, and I had refused, flatly. And the more I refused her, to break character, to go against the grain, the more intensely she put up her antics, her ostentatious threats of suicide.

I would sometimes come into the flat and see her standing in the middle of the living room, a pair of sewing scissors pointed at her wrist. *You want to see me die, is it? Is that what you want? I'll kill myself and you'll surely regret it.* I would remain absolutely still, waiting, and, sensing my inertia, my mother would make a small cut on her skin and hold the wound to my face. *See, this is what you made me do, you useless thing.*

And then she would fall to the ground, scrunch herself into a knot and burst into tears, already onto her second act. In her earlier attempts, I would run up to her, mortified with fear, and wrap her bloodied wrist with a rag, trying to calm her down. Later, as I grew older and wised up to her staged ruses, I would root myself to the spot, not budging, not relenting, as she wailed and hammered her fists to her chest, the sound of each thump meaty and hollow, beating out a steady rhythm. I would watch and study her as she put up this charade again and again, and each time, the only thing that crossed my mind was an image of something I had once seen in an animal documentary on wild gorillas, of a bereaved mother, her dead baby draped over one arm and the other madly drumming her hairy chest. From the gorilla's gaping mouth, I heard the wretched howls of my mother, shredding the air around us, pulsing with pain. What misery was I beholding, this spectacle of grief—if only I could reach out and put a stop to it, to ease the pain once and for all, permanently. And yet, stuck and paralysed, smouldering inwardly with fury, I could not—would not—do a single thing to alleviate my mother's suffering. She was only putting on an act, a very convincing one, I told myself, and I wanted nothing to do with it.

Is that why I didn't stop her when she wanted to die?

No, it's not. It just happened.

I didn't do anything.

It happened so fast. Everything.

She jumped, that was what she did in the end. She was there, sitting at the ledge of the kitchen window, screaming and screaming, and then she was gone. She fell. I saw her fall. I did not believe for even a moment that she would do it. She had always pretended to want to kill herself, but had never gone any further, never beyond a certain point. She was just doing it to get my attention, that's all. That time, I thought she would come down once she was done with her usual theatrics, moving to the next act. She had always been predictable, too easy to read. Though I did not say a word to get her off the ledge, I never took my eyes off her.

Maybe she had given herself a scare, turning to look down so suddenly, in the midst of her raving. Maybe that's how she had lost her grip on the window bar, losing her balance. She fell, and as she fell, I could hear her voice trailing softer and finally vanishing. A heavy fleshy thud rose from the ground floor of the block, coming as if from a far distance.

At the moment it happened, all I could hear was her angry voice trilling in my head, in an endless loop, her words a swirl of muddled croaks. I did not register her absence or her death at the moment, my thoughts missing several beats; perhaps I had blinked and lost sight of her somehow, perhaps she had disappeared into the bathroom. Perhaps she was still hanging on to a laundry pole, to the concrete edge, outside the windows, hanging on to dear life, waiting for me to come to her, to drag her to safety. Things could not have gone the way it did; I must have imagined it, dreamt it up. It was all in my head, this fantasy, it did not happen.

But there was now only an absence, which loomed large in the empty flat. The wan light of late afternoon streaming into the kitchen touched everything with a burnished glow. And, here was I, in the middle of the living room, alone, motionless, skinned. I did not dare to move, afraid that if I did, I might break the silence, shatter the stillness all around me; if I did not move, nothing would change, the world would remain intact, preserved. My mother alive, waiting to emerge, to make her entrance again. I stood against the roiling tides rising and crashing inside me, against the slightest movement that might change even a bit of my world.

It was the next-door neighbour, who had heard the commotion and peeked out to see my mother's body on the ground floor of the block and called the police.

Was I happy that I finally got rid of her?

I don't know what you mean.

I really don't.

What's there to be happy about?

Why would you assume that?

Everything that followed came with a swiftness that left little time or room for me to think too much or deeply about what had happened. The police, the reporters, the intrusive probing of the neighbours, the whispers and stares, the blatant finger-pointing. I floated through those days in a sticky daze, my mind perpetually clouded by a fog that never seemed to lift, dull and cottony, feeling disconnected, disoriented. Because my mother and I were estranged from the extended family—my mother had refused to have anything to do with her family, and the other relatives we had were several times removed, distant; if my father had heard the news about her death, he didn't make it known, not with a call or visit—I opted for a cremation after her body was released from the mortuary. No funeral wake at the void deck or a death notice in the papers, though I found a bouquet of yellow chrysanthemums wrapped in flimsy plastic on the doorstep shortly after, with no message or indication of who the sender was, which I immediately threw away.

After I picked up her ashes and bought a cheap ceramic urn to house it, I tucked the latter at the back of the cupboard behind a bag of my mother's clothes that I had packed to give away. To avoid the constant reminder of my mother's absence at every turn, I threw myself into the frenzy of cleaning out the whole flat, intent on clearing every bit of item and possession of my mother, which, even though she wasn't a hoarder, still came up to a sizable amount. Things I couldn't throw down the rubbish chute in the flat, I carried them over to the trash collection centre, hurling the bags into the huge metal containers. Along with my mother's belongings, I also threw out a good part of my own stuff, books and shoes and bags that I no longer wanted, remnants of a past that I had no wish to remember. As for the clothes that my mother had made for me—dresses and blouses and skirts and pants, all immaculately tailored, fitting me perfectly, now mostly worn and faded but still in good serviceable condition—I put all of them into one huge carrier bag and lugged them to the nearby Salvation Army, dumping them into one of the donation bins. In the end, amongst the very few things I kept, for reasons I couldn't quite articulate, was the old Singer sewing machine. It was a very old model, made in the seventies, the kind where you could, by lifting the side panels of the counter, tuck the whole contraption—arm and balance wheel—into its hollow belly, rendering the surface flat and unobtrusive. I wiped the Singer down one last time and gave the metal parts a good oiling with WD-40 before throwing a dust cover over it and pushing it into a corner of the living room, uncertain what I should do with it.

Done with these chores, packing my old life into boxes and bags, hidden out of sight, I made myself sit on the mattress, leaning against the wall, and watch the light come and fade, training myself not to harbour any thoughts in my head, only to breathe, and breathe again. The flat was silent throughout the day, and it was a silence I soon got used to. My life, sealed and self-contained and hermetic, a closed ecosystem of one.

My days were of course moving along without pause, exerting its own inexorable pace, disregarding anything in its way. Life has no hold on death, sweeping it clean, pushing on; grieving is a luxury afforded to the very few, an indulgent pastime I could ill afford. As I was then in the final term of my last year in design school, the exigencies of a full study load and the upcoming exams took priority over anything else in my life. No one in school knew about my mother's death, for I had kept quiet over the whole incident, the few missed days attributed to a bout of stomach flu. I quickly got back into the swing of things, diligently attending lectures and tutorials, staying back for exam preps, sometimes in study groups but mostly alone. I began to spend more time out of the flat, at the neighbourhood library or fast-food joints, revising my school work, trying not to sink under the weight of a sadness that was clutching madly at the sides of my heart. I went home only when these places closed, or when I could barely keep my eyes open, my mind heavy with fatigue, collapsing on the mattress, still wearing my shoes, dead to the world. The flat soon became a foreign, dreary place to me, where I chose to spend as little time as possible.

And so, when the man proposed to get a new place for me, several months into our affair, I had leapt at the chance to move to someplace new, away from the squalid hole of a flat where death—its persistent presence and foothold—was always present, to start a different life. And while the pregnancy was a sort of trigger for the man's proposition—we were still working out the rough edges of the decision to keep the baby then—I was more than glad to get a fresh start. The hope of all of it coming together finally—to have a family, a new place—was something that kept me going, even as I felt pulled in the other direction, towards a life of my own.

But what kind of an idea of a family was I working towards—given the state of my own relationship—the one that my mother and I had? Was it enough to have a man who loved me, who provided everything for me, and a child whom I loved with all my heart—would these be enough to bind us together, to make us a family, I often thought.

For a year after the birth of the boy, I kept up the pace of my work at the advertising agency, giving myself over to its punishing demands. I took on new projects without a word of complaint, clocking in long hours, something the man was unhappy about and often brought up with me, resulting in messy fracas and unsettling stalemates. For some time, he had tried to talk me out of keeping my job—*Why do you need to work, when I'm more than capable of providing for you and the child?*—and I had to put up a case of wanting to earn my own keep, to build a career for myself. It was too early, too easy, to give up on something that I was slowly working towards. I liked what I was doing, and found satisfaction, even a sense of pride and accomplishment, with the labour and the accompanying pains that the job entailed. To and fro we went over these quarrels with no resolution in sight, and if it were not for a persistent high fever that beset the boy for nearly a week, and which had resulted in a brief hospital stay, I would not have yielded to the man's fervent request and agreed to work as a freelancer for the time being, as a sort of compromise. Indefinitely, he told me, a feeble assurance, which I took to mean if and when he allowed me to work full-time again. To compensate me, the man fought on my behalf, securing me a high contract rate, along with the benefits of a full-timer, just as he said he would.

In the weeks that followed my decision to leave my full-time job, before the reality of taking care of a child finally hit me—the man had dismissed the nanny the week I became a freelancer—I often chose to believe it was the man's love that had motivated him to get me the best deal out of the new arrangement, and refused to succumb to the other nagging thought that he had wilily forced me into a tight, narrow hole that kept me confined, trapped at home with a child, with no way to escape. It was not easy, when days were bad, to keep my mind from wavering from one state to another, to blame the man for everything I had to endure, to demolish myself with unabating self-doubt and recrimination, for my inability to act, to say no. I had to believe the man loved me— if not, why all this? If not for the man and the boy, what else was I doing this for?

I'm not cut out to be a mother?

What's a mother then? Is there ever a perfect mother? Do you have one?

Tell me what she's like.

No?

We all learn to be mothers. I learnt to be one, a good mother.

Yes, I was, over time.

The boy's everything to me. My whole world.

It was a long trying period, the months and then the years that went into the care of the boy. As a young mother, there was never a time to let my guard down, not even for a second. My mind was always spinning with the tasks that needed to be done, the fears that lurked at every corner of my mind, the leak of time that could not be plugged, where things kept piling up and overfilling, more and more of it each day, never ceasing, and the persistent, crippling terror that one day all of it would come apart in my hands, disintegrated, destroyed. A sticky film of fatigue clung to me over time, and slowly hardened into a carapace, which I lugged around like a heavy stone from day to day. My life had shrunken to the bare essentials, responding only to the urgent and immediate—what the boy needed, what my body could do, how to keep myself constantly awake and alert.

At the end of most days, I would fall into a sleep so deep that I would sometimes wake from it with an immobilizing fear that in my negligence—perhaps I had left a pot boiling on the stove or placed a pillow too close to the boy's face—the boy had died. I would run to his bedroom and find him where I had left him, in the cot, blanket tossed aside, still sleeping, and the rupture of relief was so intense that I would burst out into sudden tears.

The unfounded fear of my imminent failure, which lurked like a prowling beast at the back of my mind, never seemed to abate or go away. Sometimes, in the mire of a terrible day, when everything seemed to go wrong, I would get flashes of visions in which I could see myself lifting the boy's body from where he had laid sleeping and found him dead, my hands wet with his blood, and I would blank out momentarily. In other visions, I would peek into the boy's cot and discover that every recognizable feature on his face had been wiped off, leaving only grey smudges that discoloured his pale skin, and he would be stretching out his tiny arms at me, scraping my face, as if he was trying hard to breathe, trying to fight against me.

These visions were a terrifying sight, and even when I surfaced from them, the hooks they left were already embedded in my mind. Where did this fear come from? Had my mother felt the same things when I was a child? Could she have known that no matter how much she had tried to keep me safe, there were still things that fell out of her control? Did she think she could have protected me from all the dangers out there—or even from her?

Sometimes, holding the boy and looking into his eyes, I would think about how his life was truly in my hands, that I was the only person who stood between his life and death, and how it was possible, with a simple decision and act, to end it all for him—it was so easy, like snapping a flower off a weak stem. Many times this thought would float through my head, and whenever it occurred, however briefly, I would renew my resolve—*no, you will live, you will not die.*

But still he died.

He ran out of the house, just like that. If only I hadn't fallen asleep.

Yes, I'd failed to keep a watch over him.

But I'd never left him out of my sight till that time.

No, I didn't let him die.

He drowned.

I was there, I saw it.

I know what I saw.

I'm telling you what I saw.

The boy had been clamouring for some time to see the man, asking to see his daddy, and had refused to listen to me. *He's very busy at work, he's got no time, he will be coming soon, stop being a nuisance*, I would tell the boy, offering a different explanation each time. And when he became too whiny and flustered, getting on my nerves, I would drag him into his room and lock him there. He would kick up a storm, banging on the door, screaming to be let out. I would then threaten a beating if he still did not behave. This went on every day that week. I was at my wits' end, whittled down to the bone. Perhaps he was looking forward to getting something from the man—the boy had been promised an Optimus Prime figurine as a reward for getting a good score in an English test—or maybe he just missed him.

But what did the boy know about the man, really? A shifty, transient figure in his life, barely making a dent with his presence, here for a day then gone for the next three or four, rarely spending a weekend with the boy. Their relationship, if you could even call it that, held out only by the scantiest of conditions—a very short span of attention, an encouraging word, pocket change—which kept it going but barely. True, the man brought many gifts and presents for the boy whenever he visited, but they were nothing more than calculated means to assuage his own guilt and failings as a father. Still the boy lapped it all up, as any child would, not knowing any difference. *Can you make an effort to spend more time with him, he needs you*, I had often asked the man, straining the neediness out of my voice. *I'm trying, I'm really trying*, he would assure me, taking my hand into his, patting it, looking pleased with his efforts. After a while, I did not ask anymore.

Why?

He had stopped trying.

His other family is more important to him.

Yes, you are. We can't hold a candle to you.

Why is it so cold now?

Feel my hands. So numb, all needles.

How long have I been lying here? How long have I been talking?

What time is it now?

Time.

Why won't you tell me?

Time, the thing that we're all bound to, hanging from.

The nails that pin us to our lives, never letting us go.

Do you know what time does to us?

It eats through us. Like a rot.

We will never be rid of it.

Do you remember the day you came here? Do you remember the last time you saw them, your parents? Do you remember the last words he spoke to you? Do you remember what you said to him?

How much do you remember?

Remember, remember, as if you're the last of your kind, cursed to remember, condemned to extinction.

How would any of this save you?

To the past we go, always to the past, as if the present is nothing but a screen, breaking, broken through, perceived in passing, second by second, sucked into this infinite void of the past. Every moment is only the past waiting to happen, here now, gone now, presenting itself in your head, as thoughts, as memories, the substance by which you are bound to the things in your life.

Our minds—they're always tuned to the past, always casting a long look back. It's like the past is this great, wonderful place we had been once, barely having a chance to live it before it's gone, taken away, severed from our lives. A golden mirage, forever glowing, beckoning.

Maybe I've always lived too long in the past.

The past, the one I hold in my head, is safe, protected, a place I can always return to. Nothing there would ever change. Nothing there could hurt me again.

There, there, as if time were ever such a place, a fixed, unmoving point you can get to, to hold in sight, like a star in the sky, burning itself out.

I'm tired, so tired.

Living is exhausting, don't you think?

You got a long way to go, you're still so young.

You live, and you know.

Tell me again, what is time?

What time is it?

Ah, so late, so late.

It had never occurred to me to leave the man, not once, in all the years he was keeping me and the boy walled up in an existence apart from his other life, the one with the other woman and his child. His other family was where his heart had always been, where his true loyalties lay. The man had already made sure I knew what was involved right from the start—*you know exactly what was at stake*—and I had stuck mostly to script, not wanting to stray from it, too afraid to lose what little I had. The man loved me and I knew it—and it was enough, I told myself over and over again. His love for me was good and complete and real, and it had to be sufficient, I thought. There was nothing more to ask for—and even if there were, what was it? What had I forgotten to ask? What had I truly wanted? These questions hung in my heart, a weighty anchor, tethering me to my growing doubts, as the years sped on.

Gradually I sensed a subtle change in the man, his imperceptible waning, his growing impatience, his drawing away. At first I thought it had something to do with work or an issue with his other family that was troubling him—the acute fear of his abandonment was like a ravenous creature that crouched in the dark, waiting for an opportunity to strike, a feeling that only grew stronger with the passing years—and then I realized it was something else, something I should have sensed a long time ago.

What was it?

The man was lying to me.

I should have known what was going on, what the man was up to. How naïve of me to think that he would stay the same, to always be the man I thought he was. That I was the only one he loved or was truly devoted to—that the other woman, his wife, had not mattered at all, where it counted, not even with their child, the girl. Perhaps the man is, and has always been, true to himself, to his character, but I was too blind, too hopeless, to see it for what it was. I held blindly to his words, his promises, taking them as guarantees, tickets to a future together. Either way, he had strung me along for a long time before I eventually found out.

Yes, he has other women on the side, other affairs.

Besides me.

For years.

Fucking bastard.

The signs were there all along, which I would have seen immediately had I been more alert and attentive. The constant texting and checking of his mobile, the distracted air around him, the nights he went missing when he was supposed to spend them with me and the boy. I had always assumed it was the other family that was taking him away from us, draining his time, drawing his attention. And then one day he had carelessly left his mobile on the kitchen counter and, taking an innocuous peek after hearing the ping of an incoming text, I saw the opening lines of the message. Not from his wife, whose number he had saved as 'Wifey', but one that he had listed under a single acronym, 'A'—mine was listed as 'M' in his contacts. A string of kissing emojis, which set off an inner alarm, a flash of panic, piquing my curiosity. And then, to confirm my suspicions, I checked his mobile when he was in the shower on another occasion—I had always known the pin, his wife's birth date, memorized by rote, from sidelong glances—and the long scroll of texts told me everything I needed to know. The man was livid when he found out what I did—I left the texts as they were, the app still open, the phone on the bedside table, my irate glare at him, a cold fury seething through me, slowly brimming over—as if I were the one who had betrayed his trust, who had cheated behind his back. The nerve of him, pointing the accusation back at me, at the way I was behaving, the hysterical manner I was acting, like a bloody kid, how I had been for the past few weeks, months, sullen and erratic and temperamental, emotional, fucking emo—oh the look on me, how he could not bear the sight of me, how every glance, every smell, every word coming out of me, made him sick, sick to the core. I was so furious that I chased him out of the house after our fight, and when he texted me the next day and the many days after, I had refused to reply to any of it.

I should have cut him off a long time ago, I should have known.

What a fucking fool I was.

Once a cheat, always a cheat. It's his nature. He won't change, he never will.

Why then did I believe him?

Why do we believe anyone, really, the people we trust?

'Cause he said he loved me. Loves me.

I didn't know, I honestly didn't.

But I know I wasn't the first.

There must have been other women over the years that we were together—this was something that finally dawned on me. All the time he could not come over or said he was too busy, he was running around, behind my back—behind his wife's back—cheating on me, us, with these women—who were they? How many were there? I gnawed on this tiny scrap of knowledge like a beggar feasting on a piece of mouldy meat, filling myself up with a decay that was rotting me from the inside out. I couldn't stop this septic spread, which grew and ate into all my thoughts. I could not bear to eat or drink or sit still or do anything. For days, I went around the house in a blind daze of rage and self-pity and resentment, bumping into furniture, knocking over things, cutting myself on sharp corners. The boy must have sensed something was wrong, and did not come near to me, though I could feel him, like a shadow, hovering close to me, watching me carefully. When he started whining for the man, during one of our dinners, I slapped him across the face with such a force that it threw him out of his seat. He scurried to his room, shocked and wailing, and I went after him, my wrath finally finding an outlet of release. By the time I was done with the boy, he was cowering in a corner of his bedroom, whimpering like a dog who had been whipped to within an inch of its life, his hands wrapped around his head, his cries sounding like strangulated chokes. Surfacing from the stupor and realizing the extent of my beating, I bent to pick him up, putting all my strength into my hug, wiping away his hot tears, and cooed into his ears: *I'm sorry, mummy is so sorry, I didn't mean to do it, mummy didn't mean it, please forgive me, please forgive mummy.*

But the next day, I gave the boy yet another thrashing when he brought up the man again, briefly, timidly asking about his whereabouts, why he had not come home for so long. A long beating, and then a cooling down, patching up, contrite endearments. Where did I go, where did I disappear during such moments? I could see my whole transformation up to a point, and then—a complete blank, as if time were erased from my mind, obliterated, and afterwards, the surfacing, when I began to stir again, my consciousness throwing off the pall, kicking back into gear. Registering the boy slumped before me, at my feet, curled into himself, breathing shallow breaths. When I pressed him to me this time, my eyes cloudy with tears, he didn't lift his swollen face to me, shunning my eyes as if from the glare of a spotlight. After that, unable to tell whether I would fly into an uncontrollable rage or even be able to control the tide of my emotions, I started locking the boy up in his room whenever he made a fuss. Behind closed door, the boy would slowly calm down, fading into a deep silence, not a peep out of him, not even when the mealtimes came and went, not even when he needed to use the bathroom. At times such as these, when the whole house seemed sealed in an absolute silence, I'd forget his presence, fleetingly, as if he had never existed.

Of course, the man had tried to come over several times after a period of cooling off, assuming that I would come to my senses, letting him off the hook, but each time I would bar him at the front gates of the house, refusing him entry. *Don't do this,* the man would growl at me, gripping the grille bars, knuckles white, *you don't know what you're doing, you need me, let me in.* I held my ground for as long as I could, but already I knew I could not keep it up for long, the inordinate strain of resistance wearing me down. It was a losing battle, right from the start. The man begged to be let in, to be a part of our lives again, begged till his voice turned hoarse. He always got what he wanted and would never take no for an answer.

Yes, in the end, I gave in.

What can I do?

There's nothing else I can do.

I need him.

My life was tied so inextricably to the man that I could not imagine it without him, having depended on him in every aspect of my life: finances, security, well-being, safety, refuge. With the boy in tow, the bonds grew even more immutable, unbreakable. It was no longer just me—it was the boy too, and perhaps even more so, since he was still young and needed his father; how much he looked up to the man, how he adored him. To take this away from the boy was inconceivable—I could not possibly do this to him. What would it be like for him to be fatherless, like me? To have and to lose—no, to be abandoned by—a father at such a tender age? What would he know? Would he hate me for it?

I struggled with the knowledge of the man's infidelities—the gall of having the tables turn on me, to be the one who was cheated on, ah, the twist of karma, the unsparing hand of retribution—his duplicity, which sat like a bush of thorny weed in my gut, growing and sprouting, seizing over my thoughts, my emotions. I could not bear the idea of living with the man's lies, and yet, what other alternatives did I have—to leave him, to take the boy and go, somewhere, anywhere? But where and how, when I knew I could never cut the ties with the man, because, in a hidden, darker part of me, I still love the man. Would he ever change—and he kept assuring me that he would, for me, for the boy's sake. He would do anything to keep us together, he promised.

What does all this have to do with anything, with what I've done?

What do you mean?

Causes, consequences, don't you know? One thing follows the other. Everything is connected.

Is that why I brought you here?

Smart girl.

Maybe.

Why?

'Cause I could no longer sit there and do nothing and wait for him to tell me yet another lie.

I had to act, to let him know.

That he couldn't have everything all the time.

That he should know, for once in his life, what it feels to have something precious pried out of his hands.

By taking away what's important to him.

Yes, that's why you're here.

I would not have thought of bringing the girl here, if not for the boy's death. She is such a beautiful delicate thing, so soft, so fragile, I thought, from the numerous times I had observed her, like a petite porcelain doll. It was easy to see that the man loved the girl, from the way he would stoop to hug the girl when he picked her up from her weekend enrichment classes, the delight on his face when he played with her at the small park near where they lived, pushing her on the swing. The look on his face, how it lit up whenever she smiled or laughed or whispered into his ears. Everything he held back from the boy, he did it for the girl, openly, without reservation. It wasn't fair, of course, but there was nothing to do about it. The boy was a bastard after all, a nobody. The girl was the only child that mattered to the man, the one he truly adored, his only flesh and blood.

The plan came to me, ripe and fully formed, after I put the boy away, as if it had been working itself out in my mind all this time without my knowledge. And without any deliberation, I went straight into its execution. I was afraid that if I hesitated and tarried, I would lose the courage to do it, to accomplish what needed to be done.

What's that I needed to do?

To make the man feel how I felt, to make him see.

Why didn't I tell him about the boy? About his death?

I'm not sure it would have mattered to him.

No.

The boy was nothing to him, only an obligation, a mistake, right from the start. But not you. You're the one he loves, the one for whom he would feel the deepest loss if anything were to happen.

I had to take you away from him.

He can't have everything, not anymore.

I knew exactly what I was doing.

And I knew enough to know the exact whereabouts of the girl on weekday afternoons, for I had been tracking her for a while, memorizing her routine, her weekly schedule. I knew what she was doing at any point in time, where she was, who she was with. That day I got to the school early in a taxi and waited outside the gates for the morning-class students to be let out for the day. It was a Friday and the girl had an English enrichment class at a shopping mall a few streets away. For the past month, she had walked alone to the class; perhaps she was old enough to have this little freedom of movement, or perhaps she had asked her parents for permission and they had allowed it. After all, it's only a short distance away from the school, a ten minutes' walk, mostly covered walkways along the route.

I saw her walking out with two of her friends, and began to follow them for some distance. They were sharing a bag of gummy bears, from which the girl chose only the yellow and blue ones to eat. Flanked by the two classmates, the girl had held court, the bag of candies in her hand, dispensing them at will to her friends. At a road crossing, they parted ways and I quickly made my move, going up to the girl and began telling her the story I had concocted, that her parents had just been in a car accident, and that I, a close friend of her father, was there to take her to the hospital.

The girl had stared at me in disbelief at first, fear spreading like a fire across her face, contorting her features. When she began to look around her, as if hoping to find someone else, her maid, to confirm the news, I gently took her arm and led her to the side of the road and started flagging for a taxi. I repeated the story of her parents' accident, adding little details, refining the plot, and I could sense a slight hesitation on the girl's part as she listened, which swiftly gave way to a lowering of her guard, her arm losing resistance. A taxi came along soon enough, and we quickly got into it. And, as if she had finally allowed the news to sink in, the girl broke out in an alarming cry. The taxi driver shot a glare at me via the rear-view mirror, and I returned it in kind. I held the girl to me, putting my arm around her shoulders, and comforted her. The front and sleeves of her baby-blue school uniform slowly became damp with tears. I had the taxi driver drop us off at the main road near where I lived and, still holding the girl's hand in mine, I led her to the house.

The girl kept turning to look at me, her face stricken with dread and growing confusion, and I had to smile and assure her constantly, telling her that I needed to get something from my place for her parents before heading down to the hospital. When we stepped through the front gates of the house, something came over the girl suddenly, perhaps a realization of sorts, and she dropped her hand from mine and made a move to slip out of the gates. I immediately grabbed onto her hair and dragged her into the house. She started screaming and swinging her arms at me, and in a panic, I punched her head hard several times, which had the instant effect of silencing her and reducing her to murmuring sobs.

I hauled her to the boy's bedroom and kept her under lock. For the whole evening and into the night, she screamed and screamed, throwing things around in the room and banging on the walls. Her fury was astonishing for a girl her age, savage and unrestrained. I sat on the sofa in the living room the entire time and waited for her to deplete her rage, which I knew wouldn't last long. I just had to wait it out. When she was finally spent and became quiet behind the door, I got up and checked my comportment in the reflection in the window that had turned dark, mirrored. Then I proceeded to the room, unlocked it, went in, and started to clean up the mess. The girl was crouching beside the upturned bed, the sheet and blanket in tatters around her, staring at me with scorching hostility, her weary face etched with pain and bewilderment. *If you don't behave from now on*, I quietly told her, *you will have nothing to eat. If you don't listen, you'll get nothing from me. I'll starve you to death and if you don't believe me, go ahead, try it.* Then I killed the lights, locked the door again, and left her alone in the dark.

Ah, you still remember my face from that day?

I was only trying to make you behave.

Of course, I didn't mean any of it.

I was just very angry with you, for the mess you had made.

What did you see?

Something strange about my face?

What?

I looked, what, dead?

That's funny.

Gosh, you really thought that?

That's ridiculous.

Okay, I'll calm down.

Why is it so hard to breathe?

Why is it so dark?

What time is it?

Yes, yes, yes.

I had to keep the man away for the first few nights as a precautionary measure, texting him to let him know I had a bad flu, and that it was better for him not to visit until I recovered. He didn't reply until three days later. In any case, I did not think he would have bothered or even considered coming over with the girl's sudden disappearance. What would I not give to see the man's face during those early days, to see his panic, his desperation, his anguish. Finally, I thought, his rightful dues, it's about time.

The news of the girl's disappearance made the headlines in the Home section of the papers the very next day, as expected, as well as in a brief news segment on TV. The man's wife appeared in it, sans make-up, wearing a dark purple blouse, her hair artfully arranged, cascading over her shoulders. I studied her face as she made her statement, her eyes red and watery and firm, her stare directed straight at the viewer. Her voice when she spoke came across as weak and frail, on the verge of cracking into hysteria. *We just want her to be back safely, that we are here for her, that's all we want.* Then, as if on cue, she lifted a crumpled tissue to her eye, her mouth, blocking out the rest of her words. Where was the man, I wondered? Why had he not been the one to do this, to appear on live TV, to plead for the girl's safe return? Why had he subjected the woman to such an ordeal, to expose her vulnerability for everyone to see, to pity? The segment was over before long, barely allowing me to gain anything real or significant from it. I went online to search for the news clip afterwards, viewing it many times over, latching on the woman's every word, watching, waiting for the imminent breakdown, a bloom of disdain and gratification suffusing my insides, rising to my face, tingling my skin to a blush. How ugly the woman had looked, how contemptible, disgraceful, to display her weakness so publicly for all to see—and yet, what a thing to witness, for a creature like her to be brought to heel, to be reduced to such a state. Hadn't she, too, earned her dues, like the man, for what she had done, for taking things for granted, for assuming life would always be fair and good and unstinting, siding itself with her all the time? For her complicity, as much as for her wilful ignorance, she deserved what had come for her.

Watching the woman lose her composure again and again in these repeats, I shuddered with pleasurable jolts at the thought of the man's dwindling opinion of his own wife—what could he possibly see in her now? What would he want to do with her?

By then, I had more or less garnered a clear, workable impression of the woman, had formed an outline of her personality and character, who she was, from the things she did, her discernible traits evident in her deeds and actions, accumulated from the months of shadowing her. Her fastidiousness in her appearance, preferring the clean-cut, modest lines and silhouettes of loose, flowy dresses or skirts paired with a monochrome top or cardigan, modelled perhaps after a Japanese shufu, housewife. While patient and reserved with the wait staff at the cafes she frequented, she occasionally revealed a streak of tetchiness when driving, quick to employ the car horn at the slightest delay or inconvenience. With the girl, the woman was no less indulgent, though at times, she seemed fazed, slightly flustered by the former's childish exuberance, clamping it down with a stern look or disapproving silence whenever she misbehaved or stepped out of line. Always, on her painted face—lightly powdered with a dash of sheer lipstick, skin dewily moisturised—a serene, detached smile, and in her manners, composed and dignified, polished to a shine.

Once, on a whim to get closer to the woman, I went up and stood next to her in the snacks aisle at the Cold Storage supermarket. The air around us was perfumed with the miasma of her lotion and fragrance, dense and citrusy, a scent I was very familiar with, having sat in the man's car often enough, the unbearable smell pervading its interior. Keeping my gaze fixed on the shelves of baked pistachios and roasted macadamia nuts, I overheard her speaking to the girl, a pack of shortbread biscuits in her hand: *let's get this for daddy, okay, dear? It's his favourite.* It took every bit of my self-control at that moment not to confront her, to scream: *do you really not know, or do you simply not care, what the man is doing? What kind of woman are you to allow this? Don't you know I exist, and the boy, too?* I must have given her a certain look when I glanced over briefly, for she scrunched her brows momentarily when she glimpsed my face. I reached to the next shelf to pick up a bag of baked almonds, fixing my whole concentration on the nutrition label at the back, my eyes glazed over, my chest roiling with suppressed rage. I fled the supermarket as quickly as I could, when they moved out of the aisle, tripping over myself in haste.

And now I had the other woman's daughter with me, locked in the room. It had felt like a vindication at last, the severance of something that had been left to go on, to rot, for too long. Whatever existed for the man before—his other family, the security and status and safety that came with it and were held precious by him—was no longer there, swiftly and unexpectedly taken from him. Where could he go, who could he turn to? He had nothing now, I thought.

Why did I want to do this to him?

He deserved it.

He took away my life, everything.

He didn't care how we live or die.

He wouldn't care if the boy died.

I saw him die. I held him in my arms. I put him back together.

No, I didn't do it.

Stop saying that, it's not true.

I didn't do it for myself.

No.

I had wanted the boy to be the best thing between me and the man, something to keep us together. I loved the man and I had wanted to have a child with him, a family. A child would be a wonderful thing, a beautiful thing. Someone who took after the man, someone sweet and pure and loving and special. *The boy looks exactly like me*, the man had once said, holding the boy's sleeping head against his chest. I remembered that, and I remembered believing it was all true, that the boy was a dead ringer of the man, down to his broad forehead, large upturned eyes, and jug ears. Every time I looked at the boy, I would be reminded of the man, and I knew the decision was the right one.

To keep the child.

I didn't say I didn't want him at first.

I changed my mind.

No, I don't keep changing my story.

I get to tell my own story, not you. I get to say what's real and what's not. You don't know anything, so just shut up.

I'm getting to it.

You'll understand it later.

Why do you keep asking me about the boy?

Told you so many times. He drowned.

What else do you need to know?

Where is he now? What did I do to him?

I thought you already knew.

Ah, the boy didn't tell you.

He didn't trust you.

I won't trust you either.

I'm getting so tired now.

I don't have much time left?

What's going to happen?

I'll know soon enough?

Stop this stupid game.

The girl was always playing tricks, always coming up with new ideas to fool me. First the hide-and-seek games, and then her imaginary friend, a ruse she kept up and expected me to fall for. Did she really think I'd be duped by such childish antics, the whispered conversations behind closed door or the leering sidelong glances? I saw through her tricks every single time. Still, she made it so real, so convincing, that at times she could have me fooled, if I were a little more susceptible.

That time we were playing one of the hide-and-seek games she so loved, and I had found her in the garden, standing at the base of the mango tree, looking at something on the ground beside the exposed roots. I had searched the whole house before I finally spotted her from the windows of the master bedroom, her slight figure half-hidden in the shade of the tree. She did not show any sign of noticing my presence till I appeared before her. For a moment, surveying the immediate environs of the garden for possible escape routes, I thought the girl was thinking of ways to flee, perhaps climbing the mango tree and jumping over the brick wall—the topmost branches extended over it, and beyond that there was a narrow path that stretched along the canal, leading to the main road. A smart move, very clever of her, I thought then, something I wouldn't put it past her.

But as I came closer to her, I noticed the dirt on her hands, as if she had been clawing at the earth. Her face was calm, blank, when she turned to acknowledge me, her thin brows crooked in slight consternation, as if I had interrupted her in a private task. There was a broken stick near her feet, which I assumed she had used; the hole she had dug earlier was barely a dent that she didn't bother to hide. She held out her hands, as if she had wanted to show me something, but they were empty.

Standing in the cool shade under the tree, close to the girl, I could smell the fresh rot in the still air, the fallen mangoes littered everywhere on the ground, the skins torn and the flesh decomposing to grey mushy pulp. Were the mangoes in season again—or had they always been around, ready to be harvested? When was the last time I had stepped under the tree, or for the matter, eaten a mango? I toed a rotting mango with the tip of my slipper, mashing the juicy pulp. *What are you doing here*, I said, keeping my tone level. *He told me to find it here, he said it's just right at this spot*, she said.

I grabbed the girl by the arm and dragged her to a standing water pipe beside the bougainvillea hedge and hosed her down with a full blast. She gasped as the cold hit her full on, putting up her hands to keep the jet of water from stinging her eyes. Then, still dripping wet, I pulled her to the bedroom, threw her inside, and locked the door. She did not put up a fight, like I expected, surprisingly tame this time apart from the whimpers and soft sobbing.

Returning to the garden, I covered up the hole with a few pats of soil, and later cleared the ground of the decaying mangoes with my bare hands. The black ants and wriggling maggots, roused and confused by the disturbance, crawled up my fingers helter-skelter, and I had to flick them off from time to time, sometimes snapping their bodies into half, fragments. A full black garbage bag of mangoes that I had to haul and dump into the large bin outside the house. I had set aside two mangoes that were just about to putrefy, dark spots blotching the loose darkening skin, scooped up some of the flesh into a bowl, and brought it to the girl.

Eat it and finish it, I told her, *that's all you're going to have today.* The next day, the bowl was empty, and there was a small pool of vomit beside the bed. The girl was under the blanket, shivering and feverish, in cold sweat. *This is what happens when you behave badly, when you lie to me*, I warned her, *if you do it again, this is what you'll get.* The girl glanced at me, her eyes glazed and distant, and nodded weakly. I took the bowl away, already crawling with ants, and brought the girl a glass of warm water and half a Panadol. Later, when I touched her body, after she had fallen asleep, it had felt stiff and icy-cold, as if cast in marble.

After that, the girl was much quieter, more than usual, often refusing to come out of the bedroom, even when I left it open. She would sit at the small table, surrounded by her toys and dolls, or lie in bed, staring at the ceiling, mumbling to herself. Whenever I entered the room, she would straighten her body self-consciously and stare at me with a pointed expression, which she would later soften into a smile. I had tried to bring up the incident at the mango tree with her, but she only looked distractedly out the window as if she had not heard my question. She has always been good at pretending, and so I let her be, no point getting riled up by her behaviour. Occasionally, to remind her of what she had done, I would serve her mangoes for her meals, only this time they were the fresh ones I had plucked from the tree, topped with a splash of chocolate syrup or a dusting of rainbow sprinkles. She never touched any of it.

I wasn't trying to kill you. Why would I do that?

The look on your face every time I serve this up. Priceless.

How else can I make you learn?

It isn't that bad.

After all, you need to eat, don't you?

You'll eat, if you're hungry enough.

I doubt you'd starve.

You won't, I won't let you die.

What's the point?

I made sure to feed the girl well enough to keep her alive, two meals a day, nothing more, after the incident. The girl was listless most of the time, after her games, barely stirring from where she sat or lay, her eyes half-closed, her breaths shallow. When she could muster up the energy or interest, she would still draw, picture after picture of a house with stick figures in them, in pairs and threes. The dog was no longer in these pictures, and the sun, too, had disappeared. In place of these, there was a tall sprawling tree with yellow lumps hanging from the branches, and always, a boy standing under it, in a pair of knee-length blue shorts, and a white shirt stained with brown smears. A boy with black orbs for eyes, a thin horizontal line for a mouth, two dots for a nose. A new trick, perhaps, to get to me—where did she even get the idea? I didn't give these drawings more than a quick glance, sensing the girl's eyes on me when I looked at them, not wanting to give her the satisfaction of my curiosity, my apprehension. Instead, I would beam at her with a full smile and praise her for her skills, for the wonderful shading of colours, so vivid, so striking. Later, after she had put away her crayons and colour pencils, I would take away these drawings, tear them up and throw them out with the garbage.

But the girl continued to draw, and in each picture, she would give the boy more details: a crown of wiry hair, a large scar across his forehead, jug ears, a bubble of light in each of his eyes. In all of them, the boy's mouth was now open, a trail of tiny diamond-shaped objects falling from it. *What are these*, I finally asked the girl. *Water*, she said. In one of her final drawings, the boy was standing in the middle of a page crayoned fully in blue, all his facial features reduced to dashes, every part of him white, uncoloured.

After that, I took away all the colouring and writing materials and drawing paper. The girl hardly put up a fight, only turned to look away, already somewhere else in her mind.

The few nights following my decision to ban the girl for drawing, I had the same dream about the boy. In it, he was alive and running about in the garden, chasing after something in the grass, bending low to examine the thing he was trying to catch. He let out a surprised cry as the insect, a grasshopper, leaped into the air and brushed against his cheek. When he saw me coming towards him, the boy was so excited that he ran towards me as fast as he could, springing right into my embrace in his final bound. I held him in my arms and kissed the top of his head. But when he tilted his face towards me, I could see that his eyes and mouth were sewn up with a thick black thread that was slowly breaking apart, ripping at the seams. From out of them, a dark viscous liquid started to leak, coursing down his face, onto my fingers, my arms, pouring and pouring as if it would never stop. The boy latched himself to my body, his arms locked across my back, keeping me rooted to the spot as I stared at him, transfixed by his changing visage as his features dissolved into a soggy mess in my hands, dripping between my fingers onto the ground, absorbed into the soil. I held on tightly to him—I wasn't about to let him go this time—as the boy slowly deliquesced before me, until there was nothing left of him.

The mornings after these dreams were the hardest, as I went about the day in a perpetual stupor, going from room to room, restless and agitated, touching everything in sight, as if searching for something that had already been lost for good. I couldn't focus and often found myself slipping into fitful daydreams that wrapped my mind in a haze. The girl, who had followed behind me one morning without my noticing, had asked me when she finally caught my attention: *Who are you talking to?* I must have stared strangely at her before she added: *Are you talking to him?* For a moment, I thought she was trying to throw me off, and perhaps ensnare me in her little fantasy, and I gave her a tight slap across the face and locked her in the room.

But the girl was stubbornly persistent, and refused to give up on her new game. Whenever I was in the bedroom with her, tidying up or changing the bedsheet, she would point something out and, apropos of nothing, say: *This is his favourite puzzle, where did you keep his Ben-10 sandals, he likes that* Berenstain Bears *book, he bumped his head on this corner of the table, didn't he?* The girl would then look at me and wait for me to respond, maintaining a stance of childish curiosity and feigned amusement. The first few times she did this, I had ignored her, and then, one day, I decided to play along. *Yes, this is his favourite shirt, he always wants to wear it to school, says it gives him superpowers,* I said. The girl smiled and nodded absent-mindedly as if what I had said was merely a confirmation of what she already knew. *What else did he tell you?* I ventured to ask. The girl glanced away for a second and said: *He says he wants to come back, but can he?*

No, I didn't believe a single word you said then. I knew you were lying.

I knew you're only making things up.

Did I always look anxious and surprised when I listened to you, when you told me the things about the boy? Was that how I looked to you?

I was just amazed at the extent you would go to make me believe you, all these childish tricks and games you came up with.

I don't believe you even for a second.

I can see right through you.

Why am I shaking?

It's so cold.

I can't move my head.

Are you still here? I can't see you.

What's going on? What's wrong with me?

I'm hurt? But how?

What happened?

Can you help me?

After I tell you the whole story?

But I've already told you everything.

What do you really want to know? About the boy? What about him?

Hasn't he already told you?

He doesn't know?

The boy took up my entire life from the moment I decided to quit my job and settle into my role as a stay-at-home mother. At first, I tried to divide my time between my freelance work and the daily handling of the boy, but as he grew, the demands seemed to multiply. Soon all my attention and energy went into caring for him full-time, and my work started to suffer. I could not concentrate for long on anything, missing deadlines, forgetting important tasks, making the same mistakes, and I was constantly frustrated by what I wasn't able to do for the boy: his runny nose, his persistent cough, his watery shit, the fevers. It was during these trying times that my mind kept wandering back to my mother, recalling her scathing, cautionary words, and I would often imagine what she would have done in my place, how she would have everything under control, in her hands—and I would feel a terrible sense of self-pity and also an irrational anger at myself for failing at the simplest of tasks. Why couldn't I do a single thing right? In the light of who I was, and the mess I had made of a role that seemed to come so naturally to other women, the spectre of my mother loomed large, sneering and mocking and making judgements, casting everything I did in deep shadows, making me question and doubt my every act, every move.

After six months, I had to finally give up my freelance work and rely fully on the man to pay for everything. It wasn't what I wanted, but I took what I could—*you're always taking the easiest way out, the most convenient, and it makes you lazy*, my mother's words, surfacing in rebuke—and tried to make peace with my decision. It was no longer possible, feasible, to have it both ways.

It wasn't easy at all for me to make these compromises. I felt more and more tied up with each step, each decision, distancing myself further and further from where I wanted to go, what I wanted to be. Did being a mother require every part of me, body and soul, a nothing-or-all deal? And hadn't I given it all up— my job, my independence, my dreams—to take care of the boy? Yet nothing seemed enough or good enough, and something was always found lacking in me: if only I had done this or considered that or planned earlier, I would have been a better mother, one more caring and in tune to his needs. This sense of despairing inadequacy, and also the darker feeling of resentment, grew and very quickly became entangled with my love for the boy, like thick choking vines intertwining, each grasping the other to survive, impossible to separate.

The days after I found out about the man's other affairs were a period of much uncertainty and anxiety. I was never in my head, though there were all sorts of thoughts running through it. I gave up eating most of the time, and was only reminded of this need when the boy asked for a snack or drink. The man texted me non-stop and came over several times, parking outside the front gate, demanding to be let in, which I refused every time. I locked myself and the boy in the house, enveloped in a hush that felt like a long, unbroken breath.

The boy must have seen all the fights between the man and I, though he mostly stayed out of sight—what did he make out of all our fights? What did he understand? He kept to his world, his own thoughts, and only started to whine after he grew tired and bored from being cooped up at home all the time, wanting to go out to the playground, the park, to see his friends, his father. *Where is he, where did he go?* the boy would ask again and again. To quell his demands and silence him, I would administer a hasty beating or a slap, causing him to scurry back to his room, to retreat further into himself. Still, he never gave up, and continued to kick up a terrible fuss each time.

That afternoon, we had left the house for a grocery run—there was nothing left to eat in the fridge, and the boy was hungry. We drove to the nearby mini-mart and I bought all the things we needed, mostly canned food, hardly any perishables. I bought the boy a cookie dough Cornetto which he ate in the car on our way home, staining the front of his white shirt. After we came back, I fell asleep in front of the TV, and the boy disappeared.

I was desperate and frantic, and went in search of him around the neighbourhood, and later found him in the canal. The boy was still alive then, his head bobbing in and out of the seething water, struggling against the sluggish push of the muddy currents. I ran up to the railings along the canal and called out to him. He must have heard me, for he swivelled his head in the direction of my voice, though his eyes were blinking rapidly, unfocused. He lifted one of his hands at me, the other holding onto something solid and hidden under the rushing water. He opened his mouth, shouted something incoherent before swallowing a gulp of water and going under for a brief moment. He did this a few more times as I stood at the edge of the canal, hesitant, undecided.

What was I waiting for? Why didn't I jump in to save him?

I don't know.

Even as I was watching the boy struggling in the water, my mind was already faraway, exiling itself from what was happening before my eyes. Nothing seemed real, as if the scene before me was something I had conjured up in my head, a dream sequence. I gazed at the boy as if he were something remote and abstract, an object that did not register anything in my head, though he could not have been more than a few metres away from me. I saw him move one of his hands above his head, frantically waving in my direction, and still I stood there and did nothing. My body simply refused to budge, to make a move.

Why did I do nothing?

Because it was hopeless.

I looked at the boy, and I suddenly realized how much he had looked like the man, and I felt an unexpected surge of revulsion and disgust, as if something foul and bitter had finally burst inside me, flooding all my senses. Every part of the man was alive in the boy's face, in his contorted, ghastly features—his lies, his betrayal, his unfaithfulness. The more I looked at the anguished face in the water, the more it transmuted itself into the face of the man, and my rising anger continued to mount, to shape itself into a deadening inertia. I could not move—no, I did not want to move. All I had wanted then was for the boy to disappear, to be taken out of my life.

Did I not love the boy?

Yes, I did. I still do.

Why did I let it happen?

Have you not understood a single thing, even now?

From the moment the thought burrowed and sank itself into my head, it was the only thing I could think of. Nothing else mattered. In my mind, the boy was the man, and vice versa, an aberrant amalgamation, an indivisible union, and in the water I saw only the man, his face wretched with the effort of keeping himself afloat, to stay alive. How he had struggled, his head tossing from side to side, madly flailing his arms about, gulping in mouthful after mouthful of water—and what a sight it was. There was nothing to describe how it'd felt to me—to see the man suffer, as he should, for all that he had done. Everything I ever had with him was being stripped off methodically, like layer after layer of dead skin—pieces of dry, ugly husk already flaking to dust—and the rage and pain that had laid dormant in my bones, from the years of believing his lies and false promises, of giving him a child, of living the stifling life of a mistress, were suddenly, urgently, thumping alive, beating out a renewed knell. In the act of staying still, by the canal, I saw clearly and vividly the vision of a life I could still salvage from what was taken from me, a new life that was gradually becoming possible, in every passing second. To let go of the man and the boy was to secure for myself a new beginning, in which I could start all over again. The feeling was real and inexplicable and exhilarating.

So I watched as the man—it was no longer the boy anymore, every feature smudged—submerged his head under the water for longer periods of time, surfacing less and less, until he finally stopped. He remained face-down in the water, his hair swaying around his head like a clump of seagrass. The sound of the passing currents continued to roar in my ears. I kept my eyes glued on the floating body, so tiny now, so frail, and waited some more, still unwilling to move. How long did I stay that way? I wasn't too sure. But when the moment broke, and my thoughts finally came around, like a returning tide, I got into the canal by climbing down the flight of concrete steps, and went for the body. I carried it back home, put it on the bed and began to clean it.

Yes, I let the boy drown.

I had no other choice.

It was forced on me.

Only at that moment, when I confused the boy with the man.

Did I know what I was doing?

I wasn't sure then.

Do you think I'm lying to you?

You're not hearing what I'm trying to tell you.

Are you listening?

For days after the boy was gone, whenever I closed my eyes, all I could hear was the sound of his death throes in the water, his voice muffled by the commotion he was creating. The sound seemed to come from afar, borne on the wind, vibrating in my ears, hollow and urgent. What did I hear in that sound? Nothing, but a deepening echo that carried the weight of a silence, and it was the silence I remembered from a different time, one that I thought I had forgotten, but was only merely hidden under the folds of my past.

What is this silence? When did I first hear it?

After my mother died. When she fell.

The day she took her life.

Yes.

What's the silence like?

Like a blank, like air.

Like something you never know existed until you hear it.

Why do I remember it?

Because it was the first time I heard, no, felt it in my life, when my mother died. As if the world had stopped breathing for a moment, and I was standing right in the middle of its absence.

And I felt it again when the boy died.

Yes.

Some things only make sense in the silence, when everything else has died down. The choices made and the lengths one had to go to keep these decisions. You beat down the other fears, you made yourself strong, invulnerable, you forged ahead. The boy was gone and the path was clear and there was only one way forward and I took that first step.

But nothing's ever gone, is it?

No.

Is the boy still here?

Why can't I see him?

I've nothing more to say.

It's over. I've told you everything.

No.

What is it you want to know?

I didn't leave anything out. All I've done is tell you the truth.

I'm so tired now.

I can't keep my eyes open.

Sometimes, late at night, I would stand in the living room with all the lights out, and wait for the silence to come. But the silence I heard on those nights was never quite the same, filled instead with the distant noises from passing traffic, the low hum of the dark currents in the canal. The rooms in the house were all so quiet, even the one in which the boy used to sleep in, and now the girl. I would wait patiently, but the silence refused to come. Still, I would stay like this for a long time and look out through the glass windows into the garden and stare at the mango tree. Against the velvety night sky, the silhouette of the tree loomed like a tract of darkness, encroaching the space around it, blocking out half the sky.

One time, I had heard a noise of a scuffle coming from the garden—a sound like something falling heavily on the ground—and gone out to check. I went up to the mango tree and looked around. Narrow slats of moonlight were seeping through the gaps between the branches, and the earth beneath my feet was soft with dampness. The droning of hidden insects drilled into my ears, insistent, machine-like. I inspected the area around the base of the tree—perhaps some animal had fallen from it—but found nothing.

When I turned around to look at the darkened house, I saw someone standing at the windows of the master bedroom—my room—on the second floor. A small solitary figure, standing just beyond the curtains, looking down at me. There was a strong irrepressible pull to the stare, as if it were silently calling out to me, trying to get my attention. While I was able to discern its outline, I could not make out its features, and my immediate thought was that the girl had escaped from her room. Yet, despite this brief alarm, I did not step out of the canopy of shadows afforded by the tree, but stood rigidly and continued looking at the figure, waiting for it to make the first move. It simply stood there, as if it were also waiting for me to emerge from the shadows. A cloying, nauseating smell—mangoes?—rose up to my nose.

Then, a flicker of movement to the right of the figure, and it turned abruptly aside to acknowledge the disturbance. Again, I could not make out what was behind the curtain, though the new presence was apparent, indisputable, a dark form slowly taking shape, pressing itself against the fabric. Their shadows merged, separated, retreated into shifting figures. Whatever it was, the new apparition, too, had directed its attention to me, its gaze and focus intense, even from behind the curtain. They were watching me, as much as I was studying them. My skin started to crawl, and my breaths became shallow. What—no, who—were they?

Breaking the inertia and forcing myself to move, I slipped out of the darkness under the mango tree, still keeping my eyes on these dark stationary figures, and ran into the house, bolted up the stairs and entered my bedroom. It was empty just as I had left it, the bed untouched, sheet pulled to the corners. There was nothing there, only a splash of blue moonlight through the gauzy curtains, and the sweet, sickening scent that I had detected earlier under the tree. I went to where they had been standing earlier, and looked down at the garden, at the tree, trying to place myself in the darkness.

I hastened to the girl's bedroom, unlocked it and peeked in. A lump under the blanket on the bed. I went up to it and shook the girl awake. She pulled back the blanket, popped her eyes wide open, and in the dim light, I saw the girl staring at me with raw puzzlement, reading my expression. I was just about to speak up, to question the girl, when I caught a whiff of the sweet smell again, and stopped short. I pushed her away and, switching on the bedside lamp, searched the room high and low for the source of that smell. But by the time I was done, the smell was already gone. The girl's eyes were on me the entire time, impassive, inscrutable.

Do I remember the smell?

Yes, always. I won't forget that smell.

Can I smell it now? Why do you ask?

I'm not sure. It's getting so hard to breathe now.

I don't know.

What have I forgotten?

Stop going around in circles, I don't want to play your games anymore.

After the incident that night, I took even greater care to observe the girl wherever she went around the house. She had quietened down significantly since the earlier days when I first brought her into the house, and, while there used to be tantrums and spells of crying and moodiness and restlessness in the past, there were now only long stretches of quiet and stillness. The girl stayed in her room most of the day, playing with the dolls, humming songs to herself, reading, daydreaming. From time to time, I would find her wandering in and out of the other rooms in the house—no, these were not the hide-and-seek games she still wanted to play—as if in a daze, pausing momentarily from some private conversation she was having when she sensed my presence. She would wait for me to acknowledge her or to issue some instructions, before withdrawing herself elsewhere. Once or twice, she would stand at the full-length windows of the living room, motionless, gazing out at the mango tree.

Occasionally, she would come to where I was and sit with me, staring at what I was doing. It was unnerving to be around her then, her scrutiny of my every move tight and severe, her placidness too frigid, too otherworldly to come from someone so young. Her stares, in such occasions, were no longer aggrieved or resentful or frightened, but pained and sad, even sorrowful, as if she were touched by some sort of new awareness, a secret knowledge. What did she know? I would smile at her—making every effort to strain the doubt out of my face, to keep my composure around her; there was no need to play into her hands—and pat her head, shoulders, and tell her to return to her room, to go and play. She would give a submissive nod, get up slowly, and leave. Back in her room, I could hear the mumbling starting up, as if she were engaged in a conversation—she tried to keep her voice low, but in a quiet house, sounds travel—though I was not able to make any heads or tails from what was been said, the threads and topics eluding me completely.

Perhaps, because of the girl's erratic behaviours, I soon took to stuffing her mouth with a wet towel and binding her hands and feet with plastic cable ties whenever the man came by for a brief visit, rare as it were—he could no longer stay the night, for the other woman, his wife, had needed him to be around all the time, though, as he claimed, they hardly talked to each other. The news of the girl's disappearance had died down barely after a week but the man was still clearly distraught by it, and angry also with the pace of the investigation, the lack of leads, and the other woman's constant cold shoulder. *She acts as if she's the only one whose child is missing, but what about me, doesn't she know how miserable I feel too, how terrible?* the man would ramble on and on during his visits. I would nod appropriately and say nothing, letting the man exhaust his tirade.

Only twice did he ask about the boy, which I was quick to give a reply: *he's at his friend's for a sleepover; he's at the school camp this week*. Beyond these perfunctory enquires, the man barely showed any other concern for the boy or his well-being, which only further convinced me to keep the news of the boy's death from the man for as long as I could. The man did not deserve to know, I felt. Sometimes, when I sat at the dining table and listened to the man berate, moan and cry over the girl's disappearance, I would start to imagine noises coming from different parts of the house, alerting him to the presence of the girl. Was the girl trying to make her presence known, to alert the man to her whereabouts? I'd prick up my ears, sifting through the random noises, attempting to isolate any that might be a dead giveaway. The looming fear of the man's sudden discovery laid like a booby trap in my mind, waiting to snap anytime.

Are you okay? the man stopped to ask once, teary-eyed, sensing my distraction. *Yes, I'm good, everything's fine*, I said, getting up from my seat at the dining table, and started keeping my hands busy with small chores around the kitchen, washing and putting away things. I offered the man more beer, more snacks, a constant bait of consolations and commiserations.

I know it's impossible to keep you here forever.

But I had to try.

Did I fail?

How did you do it? To escape from the room?

He helped you?

Who?

The boy?

Stop lying. The boy's dead.

Yes, he is. I was there when he died.

No, he's not here.

No, no, no.

I held his head down in the muddy water. I held it tight. There was a small struggle in the beginning, but it soon passed. My hand on the boy's head, my fingers gripping his soft hair, the silvery rush of water gliding across his skin on his neck, the white of his shirt coming through the surface, alive with ripples. A great churning under my hand, forcing its way up, out, but I kept my strength steady, resisting, suppressing. Then, a gradual weakening, and suddenly, after what seemed like a passage of eternity, a stillness. The silence came right after that, the silence I had once heard before, and it was calm and peaceful all around. Time started to move again, in my head, clicking its silent beats. The boy was still and quiet in my arms, as if he had fallen asleep right there in the water. When was the last time he had lain like this in my arms?

I wasn't sure how I did it, but I managed to drag the body against the flow of the rushing water and carried it out of the canal. I laid the boy down on a soggy grass patch and cleared the streaks of mud from his cold, pallid face. Nothing entered my mind, not a single thought, as I hovered over the dead body of my son. I looked around me, at the field of tall grass and the pebble-strewn path leading to the street, and felt everything—every blade of leaf, every bit of sand, the soft yield of the earth—coming loose, losing its mask of reality, as if I were stranded on a movie set, all the backdrop removed. There I was, in the midst of a scene—but who was I? What was this thing before me? And then, in a flash, I saw myself hovering at a distance, looking at the person kneeling on the ground, holding the boy's hand, and wondered for a moment whether it was possible to will myself to walk away from all this, to leave this other person behind.

Go, you don't have to stay here anymore, you're free.

The voice was clear, resolute, resounding in my head. *Go, now.*

A familiar voice, one that I heard all the time.

Still, I did not move, did not do a single thing. The lights had fled the sky, and it was getting darker by the minute. No one around, but us, the boy and I, bonded in death, as in life.

When did it occur to me to do what I did? When did the seed take hold and start to grow inside me? Perhaps it was easier, in retrospect, to supply a reason or motive for my action—I had never wanted the boy, I had only had the boy for the man's sake, I did not love the boy, I did not want to be a mother in the first place, I had never wanted this life—and even right before the very moment when the idea finally crossed indelibly, irreversibly, into reality, I was still holding out for something to take this impulse away.

But life is indifferent to all that we want. For in the narrow slip of time, between one finite point to another, when the boy was still writhing under my hand, I could have done what was the right thing to do—to save him, no, to let him live—but I had held still and done the opposite—to take away the life that I had given him. And in doing so, I knew I would get my life back, once again. I made the decision in a split second, between breaths— as if there were nothing to it, an act as simple and natural as an idle thought flitting through my mind. An idea, an action, circling back, completed, done.

Yes, I killed the boy, so that I can live.

Did I feel anything at all?

No.

Nothing. It was something that had to be done.

Why?

Because I had to. Otherwise there was no way out.

And there never seemed to be a way out for me, not when my mother was alive, when everything I did was monitored and scrutinized by her, down to the last detail. What I wore, what I ate, how I walked, how I talked, from when I was a child to my early twenties—all of it had been decided for me, tailored to my mother's wishes and demands and expectations, with nothing left to chance, nothing I could do to change it. I could not lift a finger without my mother's knowledge and interference, and the existence I had was nothing more than a stick figure in a shadow play on the wall of my mother's life, one in which I only had to play the assigned role: the obedient, dutiful daughter.

And I resented this as I grew older and had a mind of my own; the resentment sharpened and deepened over the years into a dark, pitiless core inside me. Not even when my mother threatened to kill herself, with her loud theatrics of knives and toilet bleach—nothing could weaken this core, or shake it loose from its hardened grip. And the more my mother acted out, the more resolved I was to never display any weakness before her, or reveal any part of me that might betray my inner mutiny. I swore to build a life for myself when the time came, even while I was living a shadow existence, secretly, under my skin.

And I saw my chance that day when my mother threatened to jump from the flat. It presented itself, readily, openly, in a flash of a thought, right before my eyes, my mother sitting on the edge of the kitchen window, trying to keep her balance even while she was screaming at me, her hands fluttering around her face. I could not hear a single word she was yelling at me, though I could not have been more than an arm's length away. My mind was quiet except for a lone thought chasing its own tail, looping around and around. I watched my mother as she shifted her weight on the ledge, looking down her shoulder, her attention momentarily distracted. It was then, at the very moment she was trying to regain her balance that I took a step forward and gave her a hard shove.

In that instant, perhaps realizing my intention, a sudden fear swept across my mother's panicked face, and just as she was about to extend her hand to me—for help? to slap me?—I pushed her again, this time putting every bit of strength into it. Her stumpy body tilted backwards, slipping out of the window, followed by her legs, and then she was falling through the air, a scream trailing after her. A dull leaden thud rose from the ground floor, a smacking of flesh against hard ground. The scream was abruptly cut off. The whole neighbourhood suddenly seemed muted, as if holding in a long, bated breath—no sounds, not even a bird call—and then came the silence.

Yes, that was when I first heard it.

The silence, the deep, unbroken silence.

How pure it was, how comforting.

It makes everything clearer.

Yes, a push was all it took to sever the ties between my mother and I, everything that had bound me to her for so long—one hard push.

I can't go on anymore.

I don't have anything else to say. I told you everything.

My throat's very dry, I feel so thirsty.

Why? What else do you need to know?

Haven't you heard enough? What else is there to know?

The rest of the story?

Why the man, too?

What about the man?

I don't remember anything.

I don't know what you're talking about. I'm very tired. I need to rest.

I know time's running out.

I don't have to stay. I can go anytime. I can't keep awake anymore.

What else do you need me for?

What's going to happen next?

What are you going to do?

What's going to happen to me?

Talk to me.

Why are you so quiet all of a sudden?

Where are you?

I still talked to her, my mother, even after she was dead. Her voice would seek me out, and I would answer her, and we would have long conversations about the past, about her life, about mine, about the boy. I'd ask for advice and she would offer reminders, remedies, possibilities. In these conversations, my mother was firm and unswerving, as she was when she was still alive, and though her words carried a certain weight and forcefulness, they lacked their former spite and malevolence, as if she had somehow mellowed in my mind. I listened to what she had to say most of the time, no longer with a guarded defensiveness or rancour but with a placid, unmediated keenness, as if I were a child again, lying in her lap, listening to her stories.

Whenever she spoke to me, I could feel her words skittering across my body like a pair of invisible hands stroking my head, my face, and I would lean into her touch, palpable like a spot of warm light gliding over my skin. How easy she seemed—how unlike her old self—so gentle, so kind, and how quickly I submitted myself to her, again and again, with no resistance. It did not matter what I had felt and known and done back then—the past was many worlds apart, distant and barren, untouchable—we were starting all over again, my mother and I, starting a new beginning, holding nothing back. Everything was possible, wide-open, boundless.

She spoke to me about the boy and the man, and I told her everything, every detail of our lives. She only asked that I listen to her, to follow everything she said, that it was important that I did the things she told me, that it was no time for regret or remorse or anything, that I had to pull myself together. It was for my own good, my future, that was all she really cared about. What was done was already in the past, and nothing could change that, she reminded me. What I still had was in my hands, was still yet to be.

Of course, it's my mother's voice I hear.

It's her, I know it. I've known it all my life.

She's always with me. She will never leave me.

She loves me.

A mother never leaves her child alone.

No, I didn't make it up.

Yes, I hear her, I know her voice. I hear her all the time.

What is she telling me, right now?

I don't know.

Is she here now?

No.

We are the only ones here.

No?

What's that sound?

It's getting so loud.

Did you hear it?

It's coming from the man?

Is he here?

Is he okay?

What happened to him?

I need to know.

Where is he?

Tell me.

Why are you so quiet again?

Stop hiding your face from me.

I want to see you.

I can't see you.

The man had wanted to tell me something in person. He had sounded nervous on the phone, his voice breaking up at times. I arranged a time with him and waited for him by the gates of the house. The moment I saw him stepping out of the car, I could tell that he was very agitated, visibly troubled. He did not look me in the eye when he strode briskly into the house, shoving past me, brushing coldly against my shoulder. I followed suit and closed the front door, locking it. Pausing at the kitchen island, the man put a hand on the marble top, as if to steady himself, and swept his glance around the place. The kitchen was spotless, not a thing out of place. I had spent the entire day after the call cleaning up the house. The air smelled citrusy, the lingering scent of the floor cleaner. The girl was in her room, neatly gagged and bound.

I offered the man a glass of water, but he shook his head violently, declining. His eyes were roving from cabinet to drawer to hob, seemingly unable to stay still. I stood at the opposite end of the island, waiting for the man to speak. Prompted by a sudden urge, he swept his hand across the surface of the counter top and sent a glass bowl of mangoes, recently plucked, crashing to the floor. *The bitch*, he screamed, *she wants to leave me, she wants a divorce.*

Ah, you could hear him all the way from your room?

Yes, he's very angry.

What did he want?

To put a stop to everything.

To the other woman leaving him.

Was I happy to hear that?

I don't know.

I don't know what to feel.

How should I feel?

Unable to contain himself, the man started pacing the kitchen, like a trapped wounded beast, the words tumbling out of his mouth in a torrent, foaming at the corners. Then suddenly, as if he could not stand to be in the same room as me, he took off up the stairs, his steps heavy and loud, heading for our bedroom. I went after him, but hung back at the entrance, unsure whether he wanted me there. I did not say anything as the man went into a renewed tirade, his rage intensifying with every word he spewed. *That fucking woman, doesn't she know what I've done for her over the years, doesn't she care about anything I did?* I made no attempt to stop him, my mind falling back into a kind of trance, not registering anything the man was saying. I watched him gesticulating with wild, animated movements, his eyes alit with wet fury, as if I were watching a scene from a foreign show in a different language, each word signalling something that was lost on me. The bedroom started to shrink around me, every item hovering at the edge of my vision reduced to dark blurry smears. It took a long time, glancing at the closed windows behind the man, to recognize the person in the pale reflection was me, a vague figure surfacing from the depth. And when I did, I could not tear my eyes away. Who was she, this person glaring back at me? What was she looking at?

At one point, the man stopped, turned to look at what I was staring at, and yelled: *What is there? What the fuck are you looking at? What's wrong with you?* I closed my eyes, blocking out the image of that other woman in the reflection, and, with a calm voice, said: *Nothing.*

The man started to cool down after that, his anger waning, depleted. He hobbled to the edge of the bed and sat on it, covering his face with his palms. He sighed deeply a few times, as if purging his body of something foul, undesirable. I sat down beside him and brought my hand over his, keeping it still against mine, easing the tension in his knuckles. The man leant into me, sinking his head onto my shoulder, and sobbed.

It was then, when silence was slowly restoring itself in the room, that I saw a slight movement out of the corner of my eye, and looked up. There, just inside the door, was the girl, materializing out of thin air, like an apparition.

The man, sensing the sudden stiffening of my body, had also looked up. He stared at the girl, and then at me, his bewildered face moving swiftly across different terrains of expressions, all at once: shock, fear, disbelief, doubt, anguish. He released my hand and stood up, hovering in hesitation. The girl took a tiny step into the room, and the man went up immediately to claim her in his outstretched arms, letting out a suppressed cry.

I continued to sit on the bed, my body gone numb, deadened, my mind tipping into a black, silenced void.

There was a look on the girl's face I had not seen before, a deep and measured calmness that radiated from her as she stared at me across the man's shoulder. Her eyes registered a dark menace, leeched of their usual feral uncertainty, and her lips were on the verge of breaking out into a tiny smile, or scowl. In the looks that passed between us, I was vaguely reminded of a creature rising from a dark swamp, turning its primordial gaze on the world.

And then the girl tilted her head, lifting her chin, and in that small deliberate movement, my initial impression gave way to something faintly recalled, a tainted memory, a familiar gesture taken from another time, imitated from another person—but who?

The man turned to me, a new hardness setting in his wet eyes, and I could tell he was still working out the emotions that were passing through him, undecided on how to respond or act. His mouth trembled with the words he was still forming on the tip of his tongue. He pulled the girl closer to him, moved her to behind him, as if wanting to shield her from me.

What's going on here, he finally uttered, *did you do this? Why? Are you fucking out of your mind? What were you thinking?*

I rose to my feet, unsteadily, and found myself unable to take a single step, paralysed.

Don't just stand there like a bloody fool, do something, a voice broke into my head—my mother's.

The air clotted around me, making it hard to breathe. The bedroom shrank, became even smaller, a tiny cave in which all of us were made to take refuge, and every movement, even the raising of my hands or the opening of my mouth, took a tremendous, insurmountable effort. The man took a few steps back, his body tensing visibly.

You're fucking crazy, he said, *you're fucking nuts.*

Then, turning back to the girl, the man took her hand and made to leave the room, but the girl remained stiff, immobile, and continued to stare at me.

Let's go, the man yelled, and forcibly dragged the girl out of the room. I broke from my reverie, ran up to the girl and grabbed her other hand, holding on to it tightly. It was cold, clammy, as if chiselled out of ice. The girl opened her mouth, but nothing came out of it. The man shoved me hard on the shoulder, knocking me to the ground.

Don't do this, I begged, silently, a brief look passing between us, *don't do this to us.*

The man ignored my plea, turning his back on me, pulling the girl harshly along.

In that moment, something flicked inside me, a flare coming alive, galvanizing. I rose out of myself, as if severed from my body, which now lay discarded, useless, at my feet, and went in pursuit of the man and the girl.

Why did I do it?

Of course I know I can't stop him.

I know he already hates me.

I know he will leave me for good.

There's no way to stop anything.

I no longer exist in his eyes.

I'm nothing.

No, you got it all wrong.

I was only trying to stop him for a second.

I was only trying to make him stay, to make him come to his senses.

No, I don't know.

I don't remember now.

There she was again, my mother, sitting on the window ledge, her feet dangling off the floor. Her angry words floating to me, like a dream, vague and weightless, impressing themselves on my skin, like warm strobes of light. *You can never do anything right, you're so useless, you'll be your own ruin.*

And my hand touching her chest, for a moment. A push. It was nothing, it felt like nothing. And then the fall, always the fall. I see it in my mind all the time. My mother plunging through the air, her frightened voice reaching into me, crawling at the walls of my mind. They never ceased; the screams never stopped.

No, I've to listen to her.

She's my mother, she knows what's best for me.

She knows I need her.

She's always with me.

I know she can still hear me.

Like the boy. He's here, I know he can hear me too.

Don't go.

What's going on?

Who?

Are they coming?

Who will be here soon?

Do I have to go?

I don't want to go.

Stay with me.

I have a choice.

Don't make me go.

You can help me.

Please help me.

Always, in my dreams, I see her falling, tumbling from a great height in the sky, her body wheeling in the air, like a fish thrown out of water. A dark, twisting speck in the infinite sky, a celestial body, arcing through time, burning itself out. And in these visions, my mother never once hit the ground, for there was no ground to land on, only an endless expanse of space. And if she should ever land, I wondered, who was there to catch her?

No, I'm not rambling.

I'm telling you what's in my head.

I'm telling you what I'm seeing, hearing.

I'm not done yet.

The man had promised to love me for as long as we lived, and I had held fast to that promise. I was the only one that mattered, should have mattered, but the man had forgotten, he did not care anymore. I only wanted to make him care again, to make him remember. That's all I had been doing all along: to get his attention, to get him to see what he had forgotten, that I still love him. If I did not get through to him now, it would be too late.

No, I'm not lying.

There's always a part of me that hates the man.

But I love him just as well.

Does it mean anything at all?

Does it make any sense to you?

He is all I have—all I have left.

I only wanted to punish him, to hurt him, for a short while.

For him to realize his mistake. I only wanted him to come back to me, to love me.

I know what I've done.

But I love him still.

Yes, this is love. What else could it be?

He's not gone.

I know he's still around.

I know he's here.

That smell in the air, I know it's him.

The push, the fall—my mother's face slipping away, dissolving into the air. In its place, the boy's face, rising from the water, his eyes stitched shut. Then, in the next moment, breaking the threads, his eyes shuddered back to life, and in his glare, wide and accusing, as if he were seeing right through me, I saw the utter helplessness and rage. His jaws fell open, and from the dark hole of his mouth poured a river of snakes, each snapping alive, reaching for me. When I blinked again, the boy vanished, and in my hands, the phantom weight of his absence, heavy like a bag of bones.

And the man—where was he? Where was he in all this?

There, at the edge of my vision, I could see his outline, a web of shadows punched out of the dark. I could not make out anything else. I called out to him, soft at first, and then louder. *Come here, I'm here, please come back to me.* He did not move. Was he even there? Or was I just calling out into the silence?

What should I remember then?

What have I forgotten?

I'm not too sure.

What is it that I'm not seeing?

Caught up to the man at the staircase landing, I put a hand on his arm and dug my nails into his flesh, drawing blood. His face registered a new surprise, at my boldness. He slapped my hand away and shoved me aside. I hit the wall and bit my tongue, a burst of blood exploding inside my mouth. It tasted like a rusty coin, mixing into my saliva. I forced the words out of my mouth—a flock of ravens let loose.

Where are we now?

What time is it?

Come closer, I can't see you.

Are you there?

Did you see everything?

How did you leave the room?

The boy helped you?

No, it's not true, stop your fucking nonsense.

He said it was time? For what?

He's dead, he has been dead a long time.

He couldn't possibly have helped you.

Why did you listen to him?

He's dead, he's not real.

You're making him up, you fucking liar.

I don't believe a word you're saying.

I fed you, I kept you safe. You're safe here with me.

What did he say to you?

Why did he ask you to keep quiet?

He said to hold his hands?

Why're you so scared?

Why?

He's not himself? Did he change? His voice? His eyes?

What happened, why're they so different?

You stupid, stupid girl. You didn't have to listen to him.

He wasn't helping you.

What did he make you do?

You held his hands?

That's all?

What else did he do?

You held his hands, and?

Speak up.

What happened?

Tell me.

You finally heard his voice?

What do you mean, inside you?

No, no, you're making all this up. Nothing is true.

How do you expect me to believe you?

Because you're not real.

I charged at the man again and gave him a hard push. He stumbled at the top of the stairs for a second, then fell backwards, his whole body tipping in the air. I heard the juicy smack of his head hitting the edge of the marble step, like a piece of meat thrown on a slab. I froze on the spot, and did not—could not— look down at the man.

And as I was standing there, motionless, the girl suddenly appeared beside me, out of nowhere. She slipped her small hand into mine, as if it were the most natural thing to do. Roused by her touch, I glanced down, only to be met straight in the eye by the girl's cold, impassive gaze. Straining her lips, she started making a strange, strangulated sound.

Mama.

My head began to swim. I could not form a single clear thought. The girl held her stare and continued to make that strange ugly noise, her voice crawling into my ears, spreading its dark tentacles. She grabbed both my hands and pulled me low to the ground, putting her lips to my left ear, and whispered.

Did I hear him?

The boy?

Did I hear what he's saying?

I don't understand.

It wasn't him.

What did he want?

I don't know, I don't know.

My head hurts. Please stop asking me.

It's not him.

The girl clung to me, her words a snake coiling around my heart, squeezing and squeezing, tightening. I could not breathe; yet there was no possibility of letting go. What was she saying? The girl was clinging so tightly to me that I was taking in every breath she exhaled, each breath a swipe of razors. In her eyes, there was a hunger and a fire, raw and burning. I tried pushing her away, but her hands were holding mine, still gripping.

Why did you do that?

I know it's you, pretending again.

No, don't lie.

Who else could it be?

The boy?

What did he tell me?

Why do you need to know?

No, I heard nothing.

Because that's nothing to hear.

I slammed my body against the girl, and yet I still could not shake her off. Her grip on me was getting tighter, as if her flesh had melded into mine, becoming a dead tangle. I had to get rid of her, I had to cut her off.

You'll never be rid of me.

My mother's voice.

Again, I saw her fall, her voice cutting off mid-sentence, her legs kicking in the air, and then she's gone. A spike through my body.

I wrenched my hands out of the girl's grasp, leaving deep scratches on her palms and hands, and fell hard onto the floor. I writhed to get away from the girl, from my mother. I staggered to my feet, tottering towards the stairs. The girl reared her head at me, her eyes pleading, beseeching—what did she want? What the fuck could she possibly want from me? She's not real, I thought, she can't be real, I must have made her up, somehow.

I'm not raving.

I can't hold still.

It's too cold.

Where are they?

The boy, the man, my mother.

Are they here?

Why can't I see them?

Soon?

Please let me see them.

Will you?

Perched at the edge of the stairs, fending off the girl, who was still reaching out to me, her fingers like claws, leaving their marks on me. I held myself perfectly still for a second.

And then, a push.

And I was off the ground.

And there, in my flight, I saw my mother, and I was her, and I was in every word she had ever uttered, and I was in her, filling every part of her. My mother inside me, for as long as I was falling.

Are you here?

I can smell you.

That sweet, sweet smell.

It's everywhere.

Can you hear me?

Why the silence now?

Talk to me.

Who's coming?

Soon?

Am I leaving?

Where are you going?

Is the boy with you?

And the man?

He's gone? Where?

Who's this?

What do you want?

Where's the girl? Where did she go?

Where can I go?

Don't be angry. Don't cry.

Where do you want to go? What do you want me to do?

Here?

Inside?

Why can't you get in?

I don't know.

I can't keep my eyes open.

The words are cold in my mouth.

Is it time?

Can I see you?

Now, please.

Hold out my hands?

Why?

Hold your hands?

They're so cold, so tiny.

Don't let go.

Don't let me go.

I can see the mango tree, its wide green branches spreading out, sprawling over the house, blocking out the sky, the sunlight. I'm back in the garden, my bare feet on the soft grass, and I'm walking towards the shade of the tree. The warm air moves around me, carrying the sweet smell to my nose. I kneel at the exposed, tangled roots of the tree and touch the damp earth with my hands. I begin to dig. The ground suddenly trembles and the roots start to expand and split apart, opening up a hole in the ground that widens and deepens. I peek into the pitch black hole, inhaling the loamy air—it's hard to gauge how deep it is, the light barely penetrating the surface. I lower my legs, find a foothold at the edge of the hole, and step in.

There seems to be no end in sight as I descend further into the ground. The air begins to cool, the chill pricking my skin, raising tiny bumps. Venturing deeper, I can smell the dank earth all around me, the soil-packed walls humming with noise and movements, coming from every direction, thriving, vibrant with ticking life. When I pause to glance up, to judge how far I've come, I see only a pinprick of light above me, as if the ground is slowly closing itself up, sealing me off from the world. Soon, I will be in total darkness, but still I do not feel anything—no fear, no alarm, nothing.

And then I'm suddenly on solid ground, stumbling, losing my footing. Rendered sightless, I move my feet and hands in front of me, trying to determine my bearing. What appears before me, as I feel along the solid wall in front of me, is a heavy door with a metal knob at waist-height. Without hesitating, I turn the knob and slowly enter through the door. What I see as I enter is a dimly lit low-ceilinged room, the only illumination provided by the solitary lamp placed in the centre of a long wooden table. Shadows wallpaper the sides of the room, casting dark forms, flickering with feral agitation. As my vision adjusts to the dark interior, my eyes gradually pick out a figure sitting at the far end of the table. I step up to take a closer look, and then I recognize who it is: the boy.

He is seated on a small chair, watching me with a quiet steady gaze. When he catches my eye, his face immediately lights up with delight, as if he's been expecting to see me. He motions to me to take the chair next to him. I walk up and sit down as instructed, never lifting my sight from him. On his guileless face, a faint trace of sadness underlies the current of emotions straining his features. No wounds or scars anywhere, perfect as the day he was born.

The boy smiles at me, and then reaches out to pick up a mango from a bowl on the table. The mango is twice the size of his tiny hands. He starts to peel it, first by sinking his thumb into the flesh to make a tiny hole, and then working outwards, one shred at a time. The skin falls from the flesh, in long petals, releasing a dense, sweet smell. The juice, gold and molten and sparkling, falls off the boy's fingers, onto his arms and legs. He does not seem to notice or mind. The flesh of the mango, after it is peeled, glistens wetly in the glow of the amber light, like a freshly harvested heart, ripped from a body, throbbing weakly in the boy's grip.

The boy lifts the mango to my face, an offering, silently nudging me. Without a word, I take a small tentative bite, then another, the sweet juice running down my chin. The flesh tastes warm in my mouth. I can't remember tasting anything so good in my whole life. I bite off more, and begin to eat without restraint, swallowing every morsel with barely a chew. A new hunger, rising inside me, intense and voracious, craving.

I've nearly gnawed the mango down to the core when my lips brush against the boy's soft fingers. I start to lick the juice off them, one by one. The boy lets out a burst of giggles, but continues to hold out the mango. I go from licking his hand down to his arm, taking my time, savouring every drop of juice on his skin. The boy twitches, trying to suppress his giggles as I move my tongue across his skin, his mouth trembling with pleasure. I bite lightly on his forearm, nibbling, gently sinking my teeth into it. I can feel the warm heat of his skin. The boy holds absolutely still, a look of eager anticipation on his face, as if he's waiting for me to do more.

Go ahead, the boy's eyes seem to implore, *don't be afraid.*

And just as I'm about to take a real good bite at him, there is a knock on the door at the other end of the room. Have I imagined it? I listen. There, the knock again, followed by a moment of silence. Then, another knock.

I look at the boy. He shrugs and lowers the hand that is holding the core of the mango, placing it back into the bowl. We exchange silent stares. Then I get up from the table and walk to the door. I glance back at the boy. He looks at me, and nods.

I open the door, and there it is.

Are you still with me?

Don't be afraid.

Come closer.

Stay with me.

Don't go.

Can you hold my hands?

Are you there?